Sprinkled with Love

Sprinkled with Love

A Bachelor Bake-Off Romance

Jennifer Faye

TULE
PUBLISHING

Dedication

To my family without whom this book wouldn't have been possible. You all are amazing!!!

And a big thank you to the Tule team for helping to make my Tule debut wonderful!

Chapter One

A GUST OF frigid air rushed inside the warm interior of Jillian Parker's cozy garage apartment. With it being January, Old Man Winter had taken a firm hold on the small town of Marietta, Montana. And it wasn't looking to let up anytime soon.

"Thank you for watching Romeo, dear," Jillian's mother said as she stepped inside and pushed the door shut.

"No problem." Jillian glanced up from where she stood in the galley kitchen of her recently remodeled apartment situated behind her mother's house. She'd just pulled two mini-muffin pans from the oven and placed them atop the stove to cool.

Her mother stood in the small entryway holding her newly adopted black and white cat named Romeo. Her mother hugged the tuxedo cat. It amazed Jillian how docile Romeo was in her mother's arms. It was as though he were nothing more than a plush stuffed animal.

Last week, Jillian had adopted Romeo from an animal shelter to keep her mother company. Jillian had been hoping her mother would fuss over the cat and worry less about her. So far her mother had managed to mother both of them without missing a beat.

Her mother tilted up her chin and sniffed the air. "Mm...what smells so good?"

"Apple cinnamon muffins I'm baking for tomorrow's grand opening."

Tomorrow all of her carefully laid plans would become a reality. Not only did she have an online business for her handmade jewelry, but now she'd also have a physical store where she could sell her designs and have a dedicated work space.

"I'm so excited for you. I've been spreading the word about the opening," her mother said. "Hopefully you'll have a big turnout."

"That's what Suzanna and I are hoping for." Suzanna was Jillian's best friend. With each of them being artsy, they'd decided to pool their resources and go into business together.

Her mother smiled. "I'm so glad you moved in here. Now I get to see you all of the time."

"You make it sound like I lived so far away. I was just on the other side of Marietta. It was within walking distance."

"Still, this is so much better. And it makes it convenient for you to watch Romeo. I didn't want him to feel like I was abandoning him by leaving him home alone."

"Mom, you do know he's a cat, right?"

Her mother shrugged. "It doesn't mean he doesn't have feelings too. So thank you."

"I don't mind. I didn't have anything else planned for this evening."

"You know if you hadn't broken up with Glenn, you'd have plenty to keep you occupied—"

"Mom, we talked about this already. It's over. End of story."

Her mother arched a brow before she placed the cat on the floor. "You know you can't always be so picky. If you ever want a family, you're going to have to settle down with someone."

This was the same thing her mother had been telling her for the past two years, ever since her twenty-fifth birthday. All of her friends and cousins were getting married and settling down. And with her cousin's wedding the following weekend, her mother was campaigning more ardently than normal for Jillian to find a significant other.

She knew her mother's ultimate hope was for grandkids, but Jillian wasn't sure that was ever going to happen. Right now, her focus was on her business—a business that fulfilled her and gave her a sense of accomplishment.

"Mom, I know you're worried, but don't be. I'm happy."

"I just don't want to see you grow old alone. It isn't all it's cracked up to be."

In that moment, Jillian's frustrations with her mother ceased. She realized just how lonely her mother was without her father. Even though it'd been more than five years, her mother hadn't moved on. Every time Jillian prompted her mother to start dating, she would resist. Her mother kept saying that Jillian's father was the love of her life. Jillian couldn't help but wonder what that sort of love must be like.

So far, Jillian had dated a guy who was more like a kid than a man. Then there was the guy who wanted to jump the gun and talk about marriage on their second date. *Their second date? Really?*

And the latest had been Glenn. He had seemed like such a nice guy, but he just couldn't understand Jillian's need to build a successful business. And he definitely didn't approve of the long hours she spent filling online jewelry orders and building up her inventory for the grand opening.

So for now, she'd written off guys in order to focus on her career.

"Don't worry, Mom. I'm doing what I love."

Her mother walked up to her and pressed a hand to her arm. "I know you're really enjoying your business, and I'm so happy for you. Your father would have been so proud. But someday you'll come home and find that you have no one to share your day, celebrate your accomplishments, or hold you when life doesn't go as planned. Just remember, life is all about balance, my dear. It can be tricky, but if you succeed, it's the most amazing thing."

"I know, Mom." Jillian placed her hand over her mother's. "Just give me some time. After all, Glenn and I just broke up."

"That's true." Her mother withdrew her hand. She moved to where Romeo was sitting on the floor washing his paw and she leaned over to run her hand down his back. "You be a good boy."

In response, Romeo purred loudly. His paw lowered to the floor and he stretched his neck. Her mother scratched behind his ear as his golden eyes drifted halfway shut. He was such a ham. And her mother was more than happy to dote on him.

Jillian struggled to hold back a laugh. If she'd known her mother would take to having a cat this well, she would have adopted one years ago.

"Have a good time with your friends," Jillian said. "And be careful. We're supposed to get six inches of snow to-night."

"Always, dear." Her mother moved to the door and paused. "I'll be back in a couple of hours. Do you need anything while I'm out?"

"Thanks. But I've got everything covered."

"Toodles." Her mother let herself out into the frigid night.

Jillian watched as the door closed. Right now, her mother had more of a social life than she did. Still, things could definitely be worse. *But cat-sitting? Really?*

Then a worrisome thought came to her—was this a sign of things to come? She tried to imagine her life a few years from now. Would she end up a lonely spinster with a dozen cats?

Jillian watched as Romeo meandered into her black and white decorated kitchen and plopped himself on the black rug in front of the still-warm oven. He was pretty cute. She continued to watch as he washed his tail. But she was a long ways off from settling down with a bunch of furbabies. After all, she wasn't that old. And she had too many goals to accomplish.

Jillian moved toward the cat and knelt down to pet him. She started at the top of his head and worked her way down to scratch behind his ear. Romeo's purr grew louder.

"You really are a cutie." Jillian kept petting him. "But I honestly think you could have stayed home alone. I don't think you're as needy as you lead my mother to believe."

Jillian straightened and slipped on her coat. She wanted to take out the garbage before the snow got any worse. She grabbed the bag from the kitchen garbage can and opened the door of her apartment.

She turned around to pull the door shut when she caught a streak of movement out of the corner of her eye. She turned and stared into the night. As she squinted, she made out Romeo's silhouette. *Oh no!*

A pampered indoor cat wouldn't know how to take care of himself outside. He would end up lost. And to make matters worse, the temperature was below freezing. Talk about a recipe for disaster.

"Romeo! Here, kitty, kitty!"

The little scamp didn't stop. He headed straight for the road. Where was he going?

Jillian dropped the garbage and yanked the door shut before setting off, running after the cat. She'd never thought about it before, but tracking a black cat at night was definitely going to be a challenge. And she didn't even have a flashlight.

"Romeo." She strained her eyes, trying to see into the dark shadows of the evening. "Romeo, please come here." She stuffed her bare hands in her coat pockets. "Come on, kitty. It's cold out. If you come here, I have a can of tuna with your name on it."

And then she spotted the white on the tip of his tail. Romeo paused between two houses on the next street. She slowed down, not wanting to scare him. If she lost this cat, her mother would be so upset. Was it possible to be a failure at cat-sitting? It'd be just her luck to be the first. She just couldn't tell her mother that her beloved cat had run away from home. Her mother would never trust her again.

Jillian moved cautiously. She was now within two feet of Romeo. Success was within her grasp. She could feel it. She bent over to pick him up, but all she grasped was air as Romeo darted forward out of her reach.

Jillian groaned in frustration. She straightened and snuggled deeper into her winter coat. How could this cat prefer the cold to the warmth of her apartment? Cats made no sense to her.

Romeo ran out from between the two houses and headed straight for the street. He certainly seemed to know where he was going. But how was that possible when he was new to Marietta? And he was a house cat?

He paused next to a tree to sniff something. This was her chance. She moved with cautious and calculated steps. Soon she'd have that ornery cat in her arms and they'd be headed home. She rubbed her bare hands together, trying to keep them warm. Home—the thought of her cozy, warm apartment called to her.

And…

She was…

So close.

Jillian lunged for the cat, but Romeo sprang into action and dodged out into the street. Jillian glanced up just in time to see the headlights of a vehicle headed straight for Romeo.

Oh no! Her heart jumped into her throat. Romeo was so sweet. This couldn't be happening. Her mother would be devastated. Jillian would be devastated. And she would never be able to face her mother again.

Intent on preventing a tragedy, Jillian stepped into the road.

Chapter Two

*A*LMOST HOME.
    At last.

With one hand on the steering wheel, Avery Wainwright yawned and stretched, trying to ease his protesting muscles. It'd been a very long drive from the rodeo event in Colorado, but he hadn't wanted to waste money on a motel room. Now that his horse, Lucky, had been stabled at the Crooked S Ranch, this long day was almost over.

As expected on this January evening, snow blanketed most of Montana. The highways hadn't been too bad, but the side roads leading into the small town of Marietta had been coated with a layer of ice with packed snow on top of it. It was nothing he hadn't driven in hundreds of times, but tonight he was anxious to get home.

Avery had been mulling over the direction of his life. Now that he was no longer the guardian of his twin siblings, he could pick up the pieces of his dreams—of owning a ranch with plenty of land.

But to do that he needed money—something he was in

short supply of these days. After his parents had tragically died, he'd unfortunately learned that their life insurance had been minimal. Guilt and love had driven Avery to use his income combined with his savings so his siblings didn't have to go without.

Now, he was participating in every rodeo event possible in order to replenish his savings—only it was taking much longer than he'd imagined. And with his injury at the rodeo in Denver, it was going to take him that much longer to come up with the full down payment for a place of his own. His dream was to own a ranch outside of town with plenty of elbow space. And he wasn't going to let this injury keep him down for long.

His leg throbbed. The doctor had ordered him to rest it and keep it elevated. So far, Avery had done neither. Unless sitting in a pickup for hours on end counted as keeping off of it.

Other than a warm bed, there wasn't anything waiting for him in Marietta. Correction, there was Marshmallow, his sister's cat. At his request, the neighbor lady had taken in the cat and had agreed to watch over his house while he was out on the road.

Avery turned onto Collier Avenue. He was almost there. But his enthusiasm for returning home had waned in the last several months. His brother was now in the military, hoping to one day be a pilot. And his sister was away at college. Other than Marshmallow, the house would be empty—

What in the world? There was something in the road. Avery tramped on the brakes. He squinted. Between the falling snow and the long shadows of evening, he was pretty certain it was a person.

The pickup hit a patch of black ice. Though he hadn't been going very fast, the vehicle refused to stop.

Avery's heart slammed into his ribs. "Move!"

It wasn't like the person could hear him, but he felt as though he had to do something to gain their attention. The distance between them was shrinking with every beat of his heart.

Five feet.

Four…Three…Two…

And then the truck slid to a stop.

The breath that had been trapped in Avery's straining lungs rushed out. The surprise, worry, and fright all ganged up on him. In turn, anger pumped in his veins. What had this person been thinking to run out in front of a moving vehicle?

He threw the pickup into Park. Ignoring the pain from his injured leg, he alighted from the truck. "What do you think you're doing? I almost hit you—"

"You almost hit my cat."

He immediately recognized the female voice. It was Jillian. What in the world was she doing in the middle of the road in the dark?

With his heart still pounding, Avery stepped around the

front of the idling vehicle. A cold breeze rushed past him, but it wasn't enough to cool his temper. "Do you know how close you came to getting hit?"

"I had to save Romeo."

Avery shifted his weight to his good leg. "Who? I thought we were talking about a cat."

"Romeo is a cat." Jillian stepped in front of the pickup's headlights and then she lowered her hood.

His next words stuck in his throat. He hadn't seen Jillian since his brother and sister graduated high school eight or so months ago. Since then he'd been in Marietta infrequently, spending all of his time going from one rodeo to the next.

How was it possible that Jillian had grown even more beautiful? Her long hair was like spun gold and her ivory complexion was flawless. One of the things he admired about her was how she didn't hide her beauty behind a bunch of makeup. Sure, she wore a little, but not too much.

And this was the first time he'd been alone with her since she'd worked for him. Normally, he had no problem speaking to her, but suddenly things felt awkward. What was up with that?

He swallowed hard. "Are you okay?"

"Considering you almost hit me, yes. I'm fine."

"Hey, that's not fair. It's icy out here if you hadn't noticed."

"Trust me. I noticed."

Her long blond ponytail swung over her shoulder.

"Where did he go?"

Avery thought she was alone. "Where did who go?"

"Romeo."

"I didn't see a cat. I haven't seen anyone but you out here on this snowy evening."

She glanced behind her and then scanned the perimeter. "Romeo. Romeo." Worry laced her voice. "Here, boy!"

"I'm sorry." Avery meant it. He would never intentionally do anything to upset Jillian. "You know I would never hurt an animal."

She sighed. "I know. I'm just frustrated and worried."

"Since when did you get a cat? I thought you swore off them. At least that's what you said when my sister adopted Marshmallow."

"I never swore off cats. I like them. It's just—oh, never mind."

He had a feeling that she'd withheld the most interesting part of that answer, but he didn't push the subject. "So if it isn't your cat, whose is it?"

"My mother's. I was cat-sitting."

He couldn't help but smile. "Cat-sitting, huh?"

"Hey, it's not funny. My mother is visiting with Carol Bingley."

"I bet your mother comes home with some interesting stories—"

"I don't think she'll have time to repeat any gossip as she'll be too busy yelling at me for losing her cat. Speaking of which, I have to go."

Jillian attempted to step past him when she suddenly lost her balance. She let out a gasp. Avery turned just in time to catch her in his arms.

He pulled her slight form to him, crushing her soft curves against his chest. He heard the swift intake of her breath. Was it a surprised reaction? Or was it something else? Perhaps the same thing that had his pounding heartbeat echoing in his ears?

He'd never held Jillian in his arms before. Sure, he'd noticed her back in school. How could he not? She had always been and still was a knockout. But he was never around on the weekends to take her out. He'd spent all of his free time working at the Crooked S. It didn't leave much room for girls.

And then after graduation, in a split second his whole life had changed. After his parents' accident, he was left with a family to manage. That's when he'd made one of his best decisions. He'd kept Jillian on, promoting her from babysitter to housekeeper/nanny.

He still remembered the agonizing task of moving into his parents' bedroom in order to give Jillian his room to sleep in while he was away at the various rodeo competitions.

He didn't know how he'd have gotten through those rough years without her. And that's why he'd made sure to keep their relationship totally platonic. Because if they'd gotten involved and things had gone wrong, not only would he have paid the price but his brother and sister would have too when Jillian quit. The truth was he couldn't have afforded to lose her—her help that is. There had been so much more to being a guardian than he'd ever imagined.

But now that he was holding her, he was starting to realize just how much he'd missed out on. Her gentle curves fit just right against him. And she smelled so good. Was that cinnamon? And there was another scent that he couldn't quite place. His instinct was to pull her closer and take a deeper whiff of her sweet scent, but he resisted—just like he'd done for years—and just like he'd keep doing until he left Marietta for good.

When his gaze latched on to her big blue eyes, he found his pulse picking up its pace. His gaze lowered down over her pink-tinged cheeks and pert nose to her red lips that were slightly parted. In that moment, the strongest urge came over him.

He longed to kiss her. He wanted to see if her berry red lips were as sweet as they appeared. Would it be so wrong? After all, it wasn't like it would lead anywhere because soon he'd be packing up and hitting the open road—hitting rodeo after rodeo until he had enough money for his own patch of land. And the memory of Jillian's kiss would keep him warm on those long, lonely nights.

Before he could put action to his thoughts, Jillian pressed her hands to his chest. She pushed away. "Thanks. I…I stepped on a patch of ice."

He reluctantly let her go. "No problem. Just be careful. It's slick out here."

"All the more reason I have to find Romeo. Anything could happen to him. Not to mention the freezing temperature. He's not used to the snow and ice."

"Calm down. Animals are smart. He'll take care of himself. In fact, he probably already circled around and is at home waiting for you to let him inside."

Her eyes widened with hope. "Do you really think so?"

"I do. Besides, you're never going to find him out here in the dark."

She paused as though considering his words. "I suppose you're right."

"Can I give you a ride?"

She shook her head. "Thanks. I'll walk. It's just a block or so."

"Okay. Be careful. And I'll keep an eye out for—what did you call the cat?"

"Romeo. He's a tuxedo cat." When Avery sent her a puzzled look, she said, "You know, a black and white cat. He's mostly black with a bit of white on his face and chest. And the tip of his tail is white."

"Got it. I'll keep an eye out for Romeo. I'll let you know if I spot him. But he's most likely waiting at home."

"Okay. Thanks." She hesitated as though she had something else she wanted to say, but then she changed her mind and retraced her steps back to the sidewalk.

Avery ignored the throbbing pain in his leg as he watched Jillian walk away. Once more, an opportunity to kiss her had slipped through his fingers. And he had a feeling it would be his last chance. He told himself it was for the best, but it didn't assuage his disappointment.

And to top it off, he got the distinct impression he was alone in that disappointment. Where Jillian had once been overly friendly and a tad flirty, she was now more reserved.

Had she moved on? Not that there had been anything between them, but somehow when he thought of her, he imagined her as single and available. But as he relived the events of the evening, he realized there definitely was something different about her—something he couldn't quite put his finger on.

Chapter Three

*D*ON'T THINK ABOUT IT.
Just pretend it never happened.

Avery attempted to banish the memory of holding Jillian in his arms, but it was impossible. Every time he closed his eyes, she was there—all of her curvy goodness pressed to him and her sweet scent teasing him. He inwardly groaned. And then there were her big blue eyes that felt as though they could see straight through him.

Maybe he had passed up a prime opportunity with her in the past, but he'd had to. His brother and sister had needed Jillian. And as he'd played a part in their parents' deaths, it had been up to him to make sacrifices.

But that was then and this was now. His siblings were off making their way in the world and Jillian no longer worked for him. Maybe he shouldn't write her off so quickly. There was time before he left town for them to hook up and find out if those sparks could ignite into flames of passion.

The thought appealed to him—a lot. But he recalled Jillian's cooler than normal demeanor and her eagerness to pull away from him. Was it worth pursuing? Or should he leave well enough alone?

His eager imagination was getting the better of him. After all, it was good old Jillian. She was not some rodeo bunny. She was...she was Jillian.

Avery shook his head—willing the tangled web of thoughts to fade away.

He limped back to the truck. This sure wasn't the rodeo season he'd been anticipating. He thought he'd be able to brush off this injury with a long weekend at home, but the more time that passed, the more his knee ached. He was beginning to think the diagnosis of four to six weeks to recuperate might be right. Still, it beat having surgery by a long shot.

He carefully hefted himself into the driver's seat. After attaching his seat belt, he eased the truck back in gear. He gently let off the brake and crept the rest of the way home. He told himself that he was just being extra cautious as the road was treacherous. And since he was going this slow, it didn't hurt to scan the road and sidewalks for any sign of Jillian's cat. He knew it was silly. Cats could fend for themselves. If this Romeo didn't head straight home, he would find a warm spot to curl up in for the night.

Avery's destination was just a few houses up the street and there was no sign of a cat or any other living creature on this brutally cold evening. He slowed before turning into the driveway. Not exactly home sweet home. He got out and paused to grab his duffel bag from the back seat. He learned a long time ago to travel light. It made life so much easier.

Right now, he should be on his way to California for another event, not heading into this dark, empty house. There wasn't even a porch light on. That's because there wasn't a soul there to greet him. Then he thought of Marshmallow. He wondered if the cat would be happy to be back in her own house.

Avery limped up the snow-covered walk to the front steps. He grabbed the banister and hefted himself up the steps, one at a time. His injured leg protested, but he didn't let that stop him. He swung the door open and stepped inside. He dropped his duffel bag near the front door and then fumbled for the light switch before closing the door. Home at last.

Meow! Hiss! Hiss!

"Marshmallow?" Avery looked around, trying to find the unhappy feline.

It wasn't like her to put up a fuss. She was usually a very sweet-natured cat. Something must be amiss. Avery took off in the direction of his sister's bedroom. That's where the cat spent most of her time. Marshmallow really missed Beth since she went off to college. And he was proving to be a poor substitute. Perhaps it was time to consider finding Marshmallow a permanent home.

Avery flicked on the light. Immediately he spotted Marshmallow on the bed. But a movement at the foot of the bed garnered his attention. A black cat stared at him and blinked his eyes.

"Where in the world did you come from?" Avery asked the cat.

Meow.

A bit surprised by the feline's response, Avery said, "Sorry, buddy. I wish I spoke cat."

Murr. Murr.

He studied the cat for a moment. It seemed docile enough. It was definitely someone's pet. Its coat was black and white. And the tip of its tail was white. Was it possible this was Jillian's missing feline?

"Well, you certainly are a chatty one." Avery stepped further into the room. "Would you happen to be Romeo?"

The cat's ears perked up. *Murr.*

"Hmm…you must have snuck in the door when I came in." And then Avery looked at Marshmallow. "Is this your boyfriend?"

Marshmallow's eyes narrowed as though she was frowning at him. Avery couldn't help but chuckle to himself. Romeo inched closer to Marshmallow. Obviously Jillian's cat had been aptly named.

"Well, boy, it's time you went home." Avery approached the cat, who watched Avery's every move.

When Avery put out his hand to pet him, Romeo sniffed his hand. Avery ruffled the cat's shiny black coat. He wondered what Marshmallow thought of him befriending her admirer. She'd turned her head away, ignoring the entire scene.

"Hey, Romeo, if you're trying to win over Marshmallow, looks like you've got your work cut out for you."

Just then Avery went to pick up Romeo, but the cat darted away with lightning speed. The cat slipped under the bed. Avery dropped down on his good knee, bent over, and peered into the darkness. He stretched out his arm, but he couldn't reach the cat.

With a sigh, Avery stood. He pulled out his phone to call Jillian. He may not have caught the cat yet...but at least he could let her know Romeo was safe.

Jillian answered the phone in a frustrated tone. "He isn't here—"

"Because he's here."

"He is?" Her voice suddenly took on a gleeful tone. "Don't let him out of your sight. I'll be right there."

"Well, that's the problem. I can't see him or touch him. He's hiding under the bed."

"Did you say under the bed?"

"I did." He couldn't help smiling at her confusion. This evening had indeed been quite confusing. "I was hoping you could coax him out."

"But how did he end up in your house? Wait. Never mind. I'm on my way."

Avery wasn't sure seeing Jillian again was a good idea after everything that had happened earlier. But it wasn't like he was going to act on his impulses. It had been just a momentary lapse in judgment. It wouldn't happen again.

AT LAST, SOME good news.

Romeo was safe.

Jillian wasn't sure she wanted to see Avery twice in one evening. He hadn't been acting like himself. There was something about the way he talked to her. And was it her imagination or had he held her longer than necessary when she'd slipped?

Still, she didn't have any choice but to go to his place. Jillian pulled her coat back on. She grabbed her keys and purse from the kitchen counter. She assured herself that his reaction to her had been a figment of her imagination. After all, he'd had years to notice her but he never did.

Nothing had changed. And even if it had, it was too late. She'd moved on with her life. She was so over Avery Wainwright.

Now, if only she could get to Avery's house and back before her mother returned, none of this miserable experience would have to be repeated. And to think for years she'd been a nanny for Avery's younger brother and sister. Who'd have guessed watching humans would be easier than watching an ornery furbaby?

Jillian dashed out the door. This time she decided to

drive. Having grown up in Marietta, she came from hearty stock. But tonight it was just too cold out to walk. And she wasn't taking any more chances with Romeo. He was anything but the docile lap cat the shelter had portrayed him as.

Less than two minutes later, she pulled up in front of the Wainwright place. It was a bungalow house with moss green siding, white trim and a dark red front door that Jillian had always liked. The door was just the right signature touch to make the house stand out without being over the top.

Jillian exited her car and if not for the ice, she'd have run up to the front door. Not that long ago, she'd have thought nothing of letting herself in the door without knocking, but a lot had changed since those days. Now she paused and pressed her finger to the illuminated buzzer adjacent to the door.

It took a bit before the door swung open. When it did, there stood Avery, all six foot two feet of him. His brown hair was tousled and there was a hint of scruff trailing down his jaw. He'd definitely grown into a strikingly handsome man. If not for his determination to remain the bachelor cowboy, she was certain Avery could have his pick of any number of women.

Not so long ago, she'd have been one of those eligible women vying for his attention. After all, with those broad shoulders and dreamy eyes, it was hard not to fall for Avery's charms. But she'd managed to move past all of that. She was immune to him now.

As he stood in the doorway, she couldn't help but notice his clothes. She found it odd that on one of the coldest days of the year, he was standing there in nothing but a white T-shirt with a sports logo and gray sweat shorts. But it was the black knee brace that held her attention. Realizing that she was staring, she returned her gaze to his ruggedly handsome face.

"Thanks for coming over," he said. As though he didn't notice her staring, he turned to head further into the great room. "I wasn't sure how I was going to get the cat out of Beth's room with this thing on my leg." He gestured toward the brace. "It makes getting around difficult at times."

"Should you even be standing?" Her gaze returned to his knee, giving it more intense scrutiny.

"I'm not good at sitting around. I'll ice it in a little bit."

"What happened?"

"It's a partial tear of the ACL. Since I don't normally put too much strain on my knees, the doc said surgery was optional. I chose to skip it."

She nodded as though she understood. But she couldn't help but wonder if Avery was telling her the whole truth. This was the man who never stopped cowboying, even if he had the flu.

He was stubborn. It's why he'd ended up with pneumonia. That was the only thing that had stopped him in his cowboy boots. Between herself and Beth, they'd kept him on bed rest for two weeks. Amidst his protests, she'd plied him with homemade chicken noodle broth and ginger ale.

It had happened the first winter after Avery had become the twins' guardian and she'd accepted the full-time position of nanny/housekeeper. From laundry to cooking to shuttling the kids around town, she did it all. Avery had compensated her well, perhaps too well. She'd wondered how he could afford it. Any time she tried to broach the subject, he'd brushed it off. He was definitely a stubborn man.

And now, she couldn't help but wonder if Avery had selectively taken pieces of what the doctor had said about his leg and come up with his own answers, determined to get back out on the rodeo circuit ASAP. She just hoped he wouldn't pay for that stubbornness in the end. She reminded herself that it was no longer any of her concern. Avery now had his life and she had hers. Both separate and distinct. And that's how it would remain.

She glanced around the great room to see if much had changed in the year or so since she'd worked there. During the twins' senior year of high school, she'd moved out. The kids had been eighteen and not really kids anymore. She'd stopped by and checked on them when Avery was out of town, but it had been determined by the family that the twins were old enough and responsible enough to care for themselves.

Jillian scanned the living room. It was a little messier with magazines, some random articles of clothing, and a couple of coffee mugs on the coffee table. But other than that, it was how she remembered.

This room normally felt quite spacious and the vaulted ceiling made it seem even bigger. But this evening with Avery there, the room seemed to have shrunk considerably. And with a fire crackling in the fireplace, it was downright cozy. Too cozy for her comfort.

"Where is Romeo?" she asked, hoping to wrap this up quickly. She assured herself that her rush to leave had everything to do with beating her mother home and absolutely nothing to do with the sexy man standing in front of her.

"He's still in Beth's room, under her bed. You might need a broom to get him out. I can get it for you." He turned toward the kitchen.

"I don't think I'll need it." She didn't like the sound of using a broom to get Romeo moving. Hopefully she could manage with far less drastic actions.

"Are you sure?"

She nodded. "I'll just go see about getting him."

She went to move past Avery, but with him standing behind the couch, there wasn't much room between him and the wall. Not about to let on that it bothered her being this close to him, she forged ahead.

As she did, she got a whiff of his woodsy cologne. *Mm...* She kept moving, but her thoughts centered on the pleasing yet complex scent with its hints of fresh-cut cedar and other earthy tones mixed with his unique scent. It was quite a heady mixture.

Realizing she was letting her mind drift into dangerous territory, she reined it in. She focused on retrieving the cat. Knowing every inch of the house, Jillian made her way to the back bedroom. Painted in purple and trimmed in white, it too was mostly as she remembered it. A new white comforter with large purple polka dots was the only notable difference. And there on the bed sat Marshmallow on a pillow while Romeo was curled up in the middle of the bed.

"There you are. You look mighty pleased with yourself."

Romeo blinked his golden eyes.

Behind her, Jillian heard Avery's uneven footsteps. She turned to him. "I thought Romeo was hiding?"

"He was. I swear."

"Uh-huh. Then how do you explain this?" She moved aside so Avery could see both cats on the bed.

"Seems as though Romeo is making progress."

"Progress?"

Avery nodded. "It appears he has the hots for Marshmallow, but she isn't having any part of it."

Jillian's gaze moved back to the cats. Romeo had turned his head to stare at Marshmallow. If a cat could make facial expressions, then Marshmallow was definitely frowning at Romeo. Jillian couldn't hold back a laugh. This night was like one long, strange dream, ending with a budding feline romance. Is this what her life had become? Playing chaperone to cats?

"I don't think this is going to work out, buddy." Jillian moved to the bed and ran a hand over Romeo's back. And then she moved to Marshmallow and pet her. "It's okay, girl. I'll get him out of your way."

Jillian leaned forward and scooped Romeo up in her arms. He was gentle and didn't complain at all. He really was the friendliest cat.

She turned back to Avery. "Thanks so much for taking him in on this cold night."

"Actually, I didn't take him in. It would appear he let himself in." Avery smiled. "It seems he knew exactly what he wanted. I opened the door and he ran past me in the dark. I didn't even know he was here until I went to check on Marshmallow."

"But how would he know to come here? How would he know about Marshmallow?"

Avery grinned at her. "Maybe it was destiny."

"Hmpf...I doubt it. It was probably more like Marshmallow was in the front window studying the neighborhood when Romeo spotted her. After all, he's a friendly guy." She gave him a hug. "He just wanted a friend."

"Uh-huh. And how is that explanation any better than mine?"

For that she didn't really have an answer. "It was just my guess."

The fact was that once upon a time she had believed in

destiny. It's what got her through the long period of Avery not noticing her. She thought if she was patient that destiny would intervene and he'd finally open his eyes. Ha! What a dreamer she'd been. Now she was more realistic and kept her feet planted firmly on the ground.

Jillian moved to the doorway where Avery was standing. Not about to brush past him again, she paused. Once he moved, she continued on her way. When she reached the dining area, she glanced toward the kitchen where she'd spent so much time preparing meals for Avery's brother and sister.

There were drop cloths, tools, and a ladder. It stirred her curiosity. "Was there a problem in the kitchen?"

"Not really. It's just that it still had all the original appliances and décor from when my parents bought this place thirty-some years ago. So I'm updating it in my spare time."

"That's great. You always were good with your hands." And then realizing she was making excuses not to make her way out the door, she started moving again. It wasn't until she was at the front door that she paused. It would be rude to just rush off.

She turned to Avery, who was lagging behind her. "Is there anything I can get you before I leave?"

He shook his head. "I'm just going to grab an ice pack and settle down in front of the television."

Out of the corner of her eye, she noticed there was now a large-screen television mounted above the fireplace. The room had been painted a tan shade with white trim. It looked really nice. There appeared to be a number of changes afoot. She'd just been a bit nervous and missed them when she'd first arrived.

Jillian wondered why Avery was making all of these improvements. He was a cowboy from the strands of his wavy brown hair to the tips of his scuffed-up cowboy boots. She'd always thought once Beth and Jordan grew up that he would move outside of town. She wondered what kept him here in this house. It was on the tip of her tongue to ask, but she resisted the temptation. His life was none of her concern. He'd made that clear a long time ago.

She recalled when she'd finally worked up the courage to make the first move with Avery. It'd been a few years after she'd started working for him and the annual Christmas Stroll had been coming up. She recalled how nervous she'd been with her stomach tied up in knots.

And then the opportunity had presented itself. Both teenagers had been visiting friends and Avery had just returned home from working on the Crooked S. She recalled the evening with crystal clarity. A pot of stew had been simmering in the slow cooker while a fresh loaf of bread was baking in the bread machine. The laundry had been done and the house picked up. She'd waited until Avery grabbed a shower and then she'd invited him to go to the stroll with her.

At first, he hadn't said anything. She'd willed him to

agree. And then he shook his head and glanced away. He'd said it wasn't a good idea with them working together. He didn't want to mess up a good thing.

It'd hurt and things had been awkward for a while, but with time she'd accepted that it was a case of bad timing. After all, he'd never said that he wasn't interested. And so she'd waited—the kids weren't going to need her much longer.

But when he shook her hand on her last day of work for him, the message was clear. There would never be anything romantic between them. The knowledge had sliced through her heart. All of that time, he'd left her waiting and hoping. She'd felt like such a fool. It was then that she'd vowed to move on and start dating again.

She turned back to Avery. "I should go. Tomorrow's gearing up to be a big day with the grand opening."

Avery paused. Was he disappointed that she was leaving so soon? And then he said, "I hope it goes well."

"Thanks. Okay. Well, thanks again. I hope you're feeling better soon."

Once outside, she tried to shield Romeo with her coat as best she could from the cold breeze. Lucky for her, he took it all in stride. She had no problems getting Romeo in the car. She placed him on the passenger seat. As she started the engine, Romeo decided to go explore the back seat.

Jillian slowly navigated her way home over the slick roadways. When she pulled into the driveway, she glanced at her mother's house. The lights were still out. *Yes!*

Jillian smiled. She'd done it. Thanks to Avery.

Now to get Romeo inside her little apartment without any further mishaps.

Chapter Four

EARLY THE NEXT morning, Avery's phone buzzed. He checked the caller ID—it was his sister. Immediately his senses went on high alert.

He pressed the phone to his ear. "What's the matter?"

"That's some greeting," Beth grouched.

"For you to call at this hour of the morning, something has to be wrong. It's too early for class. And you aren't a morning person."

"Maybe I'm changing. You know, I'm not a kid anymore."

At least that's what she kept telling him. On the cusp of nineteen, his sister thought she had all of the answers. Maybe he had felt the same way at that age. It was hard to remember, because for him, it was a different lifetime. As for his sister, he was having a hard time letting go of the image of Beth with pigtails begging him to take her horseback riding when she was supposed to be doing her chores.

He took a sip of coffee, black with a dash of sugar. "So if nothing's wrong, why are you up so early?"

"I have an exam this morning and I wanted to review my class notes."

"And how does that translate into a phone call home?"

"I'm getting to it." She paused. "I'm coming home to take care of you."

Surely he hadn't heard her correctly. "What did you say?"

Avery clutched his cell phone to his ear with one hand while he pet Marshmallow with his other hand. They were sitting together in the living room. But his morning coffee was now forgotten as he moved into his guardian mode.

"You heard me," Beth said. "I'm coming home. Someone needs to take care of you."

"No, you're not. I'm fine."

"If you were fine, you'd still be out on the rodeo circuit."

He sighed. His little sister was not one to give in easily. She was stubborn and she liked to be right—all of the time. "I just need a little time to heal. Then I'll be good as new. The doctor said so."

"And what did he tell you?"

"I'll be starting physical therapy soon." He glanced at the hinged black brace that was strapped over his knee. "Don't worry. It's not that big of a deal."

"That's what you always say, even when you have to get fifteen stitches or have a broken arm. You know, one of these days you'll be too old for the rodeo. What are you going to do then?"

This would normally be the ideal moment for him to tell her that he was fixing up the house and then signing his portion over to her. Whereas this house fit his stylish and polished sister, it didn't work for him.

He had no intention of mentioning that the memories of their parents that were enshrined in the house only added to his guilt over the part he'd played in their parents' deaths. When he was on horseback out on the range, the guilt lightened, but in here it was inescapable—

"Avery?"

"Um…yeah?"

She paused as though considering something. "I'm worried about you."

On second thought, the conversation about the house could wait. "I told you my knee will be fine."

"But you're at home all alone. That isn't good."

"I'm never alone. I have Marshmallow."

"Uh-huh. I still think I should come home. I can arrange to do my class assignments from there—"

"Don't you dare! You're going to be the only Wainwright of our generation to graduate from college and that's not up for debate. Someone's got to take care of me in my old age."

"And at the rate you're going that will be next year."

"Hey! Have some respect for your injured big brother."

"So now you want the sympathy? I don't think so. I figured you'd fight me about coming home so I've made other arrangements for you."

Avery stopped petting the cat and sat up straight. Alarm bells rang loud and clear. His sister had tried more than once to set him up on blind dates. He'd successfully avoided all of them. He wasn't about to get caught up in Beth's match-making now.

"I'm not going on any blind dates." His tone was firm.

"Okay. But I haven't set you up."

He swallowed hard. "Then what exactly have you arranged for me?"

"Why do you sound so worried?"

"Because I am. You don't exactly have the most conservative plans. And you do know that I'm not as mobile as I'd like to be."

"You worry too much. Sometimes you act more like our father than our brother. You really need to loosen up and act your age."

In truth, he did feel quite a few years beyond his biological age. After all, he'd been a guardian to his brother and sister since they were twelve. For six years, he'd been raising them. And those teenage years were not easy. His sympathies went out to his parents over what he'd put them through. He'd had no idea of the worries that were involved in parenting. He was not planning to repeat the experience— ever.

"Enough with picking on me," he said. "What exactly have you done this time?"

"Something that will keep you from sitting at home and sulking over missing out on the rodeo—"

"Beth," he prompted. His patience was at an end.

"I entered you in the Bachelor Bake-Off."

"The what?"

"You know. The big fundraiser the town is planning."

"No. I don't know."

"How can you live there and yet I know more about the goings-on of Marietta than you do? Boy, you don't keep up on things, do you?"

"Beth."

"Well, the town wanted to do something to remember Harry Monroe. And someone donated that old run-down house beside the Chamber of Commerce, but it's going to take a lot of money to fix it up."

"Fix it up for what?"

"Harry's House. It'll be a kid's activity center. Isn't that great?"

Avery was trying to take this all in and how it involved him. "The house sounds like a great idea. I'm sure Harry would have approved."

Avery had gone to school with Harry. They'd played on some of the same sports teams. And Avery wanted to do his part for the fundraiser, but surely no one would enter him in a baking competition. He could manage cooking hot dogs and hamburgers, but cakes would push his limits.

"Beth, you surely don't expect me to bake anything that

someone would want to eat, do you?"

"You can do it. Those cupcakes you bake every year for my birthday are perfect. You can make those."

He choked down his denial. What his little sister didn't know is that those cupcakes were special ordered from the Copper Mountain Gingerbread and Dessert Company. He'd paid extra to have them use his mother's recipes—strawberry cupcakes for Beth and cinnamon apple for Jordan. And here he'd been so proud of himself that every year he'd been able to sneak them in the house. No one had ever caught on to his secret. Now it was all coming back to bite him in a big way.

"Beth, this isn't a good idea—"

"Oh." There was a distinct note of poutiness in her voice. "I thought you would have been happy to take part. Harry's family is even sponsoring you and paying your entry fee. Well, it's their grocery store that's the named sponsor, but you know what I mean."

And the pressure continued to mount. Avery cleared his throat. "Harry's family already knows about this idea?"

"Uh-huh. I was talking to Joanie on the phone when we came up with the idea. We thought that it would be perfect and her mother agreed."

Joanie was Harry's younger sister who'd tutored Beth in math for a couple of years in high school. Ever since, Beth and Joanie had been close friends despite a six-year age gap between them. Avery welcomed the friendship. Joanie was smart and had a good head on her shoulders. He figured Beth would tell Joanie things in sort of a big sister role that she wouldn't tell him.

Beth's voice was filled with emotion. "If you want to back out…I'll tell Joanie and her parents—"

"No. Don't." And then realizing what he was getting himself into, he said, "I'll do it."

"You will?" Suddenly Beth was all happy again. "I'm sure Jillian can give you some pointers. Are you sure?"

He hesitated, knowing this was his last chance to back out. "Yes. I'm sure."

He just couldn't let everyone down. But what would happen when everyone found out he couldn't bake? It would be a disaster. He wondered how much help YouTube videos would be. Probably not as much as he needed.

Speaking of Jillian, a question came to mind. "When I ran into her last night, she mentioned something about a grand opening today." He'd wanted to ask Jillian about it last night, but he got the distinct impression she expected him to know about it all already. "Do you know what she was referring to?"

"You really have been gone a lot. She's talking about her new business, Tangled Charms." Beth proceeded to give him a rundown of the handmade jewelry business.

His sister may be away at school, but she was still quite connected to Marietta. It made him even more certain he was doing the right thing by fixing the house up for her.

When she graduated college, she'd have someplace to call home.

"Beth," he said, getting her to pause to take a breath. He needed a way out because after holding Jillian in his arms and almost kissing her, it was best to keep his distance. "With all Jillian has going on, I don't think this is the right time to ask for her help."

"It'll be fine. She'll tell you if it doesn't fit in her schedule, but I don't think she'll turn you down. And if you want to win, you're going to need her help."

His sister was right about one thing. The one person who could bake the most delicious pies and cookies was Jillian Parker. For so many years, she'd helped him out with his brother and sister. She'd done a lot more than just watch them. She went above and beyond anything he'd ever asked of her. She'd been a lifesaver.

But this was different. She no longer worked for him. She had her own very full life from the sounds of it. But most of all, he noticed the easy rapport between them had become stilted and awkward.

TODAY WAS THE day.

Jillian had been waiting on this moment for almost ten very long years.

There were many days when she thought it would never

happen. But at last, her dream was about to come true. Today Tangled Charms would become more than a few doodled thoughts on a legal pad. It would be more than figures and spreadsheets. It would become a reality. Jillian hoped it was a smashing success, just like her internet business.

Jillian eased her car into a parking spot across the street from the shop. Instead of being on top of the world and walking on cloud nine, she couldn't shake the fact that Avery was back in town. Talk about running into someone—literally.

She remembered how he'd pulled her close to keep her from falling. The memory of being held in his very capable arms made her heart race. How many sleepless nights had she wondered what it would be like to be that close to Avery? Too many to count.

But that was all in the past. She was over him. And her reaction to being held in his arms, it was—it was nothing. She'd just been caught off guard. Nothing more.

Right now, she needed to concentrate on Tangled Charms—the biggest accomplishment of her life. But this wasn't just her achievement. Her best friend, Suzanna Simms, had stepped up and had helped every step of the way. Suzanna was quite the artist in her own right. She preferred to make unique charms from metal, clay, and glass. When Suzanna wasn't making charms, she was creating small, decorative figurines. Between the two of them, they'd created quite a large inventory.

Tangled Charms was strategically placed between the boutique and the hair salon. Hopefully there would be lots of curious people who would stop in and find the perfect gift for themselves or someone special.

Jillian retrieved the muffins from the back seat of her car and crossed the street. All the while, she admired the fresh coat of white paint on the outside of the building and the way the showroom stood out with white twinkle lights. They had been Suzanna's idea. The lights framed the showroom window and lined the wine-colored wooden sign that hung from a wrought-iron arm that stuck out above the front door. While the lights surrounding the sign blinked to help draw the eye, the showroom lights were static so as not to distract the eyes from the jewelry and charms that were on display.

Lots of thought had been put into the shop.

She wondered if Avery would ever visit—

Wait. Where had that thought come from? This was her big day and she was thinking about him? She gave herself a mental shake, hoping to clear her thoughts.

She was the best thing he ever passed up. It was his loss. And she wasn't looking back. She had a bright future in front of her. And she had no room in it for a romance. That had been proven by her last messy relationship.

Spotting Suzanna already inside, Jillian grabbed the brass door handle and pulled the door open. "That man can be so frustrating."

Suzanna glanced up from where she was arranging baked goods and fresh brewed coffee on a small table with a white tablecloth. "Good morning to you too. I'm guessing you didn't have such a good weekend."

"My weekend was fine until I ran into him."

Suzanna tucked a lock of her short dark hair behind her ear. "I take it Glenn was in town again."

"Glenn? Why would you think that?"

Suzanna's eyes widened. "I just thought...well, you were going on and...never mind. Who are you talking about?"

"Avery."

"Oh." Suzanna's pink glossy lips stayed in that 'O' shape as though she were surprised by this news. She held out her hand for Jillian's container of muffins.

Jillian relinquished the baked goods. "You mean you didn't hear that he arrived home last night? I didn't think anything happened around this town without everyone knowing."

"Yeah, I heard, but I didn't know you two had run into each other." Suzanna placed the muffin container off to the side of the table.

"We ran into each other all right. He practically ran me over."

Suzanna's brows rose. "Really? I can't wait to hear this."

"Hear what?"

Suzanna frowned at her. "You know, whatever he's done

now to get you all fired up."

"He didn't do anything." Suddenly she regretted bringing up the subject. She'd promised herself that she wouldn't let him get under her skin. "It's nothing."

"It sure sounded like something." Suzanna stared at her as though trying to read her mind. "Come on. Spill. It's me. We've told each other everything since we were kids."

Jillian sighed. "I did tell you the truth. Nothing happened."

"Oh, so that's the problem. Well, you know Avery, he's never one to make a move on a woman."

"Avery had an excuse after his parents died. He had to step up to be the man of the family. But then the kids grew up and still nothing. And now I'm done understanding. He can just stay on his side of Marietta and I'll stay on mine."

"You've got to be kidding, right?"

"No. I'm perfectly serious. There's no longer any reason for our lives to intertwine."

"This is Marietta. Not New York City. You know there's going to be no chance of avoiding him. Especially since he's in town for a while from what I hear. What exactly is wrong with him?"

"It's none of my business. We're practically strangers now."

Suzanna's expression said she didn't believe her. "Uh-huh. You do remember that you two have been friends since you played on the swings in elementary school?"

"Things change. People change." She really didn't want to talk about Avery any longer. "And how about you? How did your date go this weekend with the new guy?"

It was Suzanna's turn to shrug. "It was okay."

"Okay? What does that mean?"

"That he wasn't six foot two like he'd put on his online profile."

Oh no. Not good. "How tall was he?"

"Five foot six or so."

"Ouch. That's just a bit off."

"It wouldn't have been so bad if the rest of his profile was accurate, but he didn't look anything like his photo."

Jillian felt sorry for her friend. She definitely had the worst weekend. "What exactly did he look like?"

"Average."

"So then why did he lie?"

"I don't know, but it ruined any chance we might have had." Suzanna opened the container of muffins Jillian had baked.

"You should sign up for the dating service too. Then we could go out on a double date. It'd be so much more fun."

Jillian shook her head. "No way. I have a hard enough time finding a guy that I like when I meet them in real life. I don't need to guess who's being honest and who's fudging about themselves online. Besides, I've sworn off men after Glenn." She shrugged off her coat and slung it over her arm. "Would you ever trust anyone on that site again?"

Jingle. Jingle.

They both turned to the door to find not one or two customers but a half dozen curious visitors. Jillian's gaze moved to the wall clock just above the door. They were five minutes early. This had to be a good sign.

"You are open, aren't you?" Carol Bingley asked. When both Jillian and Suzanna nodded, Carol smiled. "Jillian, your mother made me promise last night that I would stop by today. And I brought some friends."

"Welcome. Come on in," Jillian said, moving behind the display counters, ready to pull out any of the merchandise for a closer look.

"We have refreshments." Suzanna gestured toward the table. "Fresh brewed coffee and hot chocolate to take the chill off the morning. And some baked goods to tempt you."

The customers all started talking at once and soon Jillian was caught up in her work. Any thoughts of Avery were pushed to the back of her mind where they belonged.

Carol approached the jewelry counter. "Everything is so beautiful. You two are quite talented." She leaned closer. "Is it all handmade?"'

Jillian smiled. "Yes."

"It must have taken you forever to create all of this."

"We've been planning this for a long time."

Carol glanced around. "It was definitely worth all of the effort."

"Thanks," Jillian said while Suzanna was off showing the

other ladies some of her colored glass charms. "So far every-thing has been a big hit on the internet. Suzanna and I were hoping that if we opened a shop in Marietta that it would catch on."

Carol moved slowly up the glass display case, hemming and hawing. And then she stopped. "Have you considered doing something for the upcoming Bake-Off?"

Jillian had heard they were doing a fundraiser in honor of a local fallen hero, Harry Monroe. Everyone in town knew him, including Jillian. He was a great guy who would have helped anyone at any time.

This past Labor Day weekend, he'd been helping an el-derly couple whose car had blown a tire. They'd pulled off on the side of the highway and while Harry was changing it, he'd been struck by a passing car. He'd lived long enough to get to the hospital, but his injuries were too extensive. They weren't able to save him. All of Marietta had been devastat-ed.

"You know, I've been giving the fundraiser some thought," Jillian said. "And I have something in mind that might appeal to everyone in town. Perhaps they could bid on it throughout the different rounds of the Bake-Off."

"Oh, I'm intrigued!" Carol took on an interested look. "What is it?"

"I don't want to say just yet, in case it doesn't work out. But I'll be sure to let you know when the plans are finalized."

Carol's smile vanished. "Are you sure you can't share it

with me? I promise I won't tell a soul."

Jillian struggled to keep a straight face as she knew Carol needed to gossip as much as she needed to breathe. "Sorry." And then anxious to change the subject, Jillian asked, "How are the plans coming for the fundraiser?"

"Really well. This Bachelor Bake-Off is going to be the talk of the town."

"I think it already is. Do you know who these lucky bachelors are going to be?"

"Not yet. The area businesses are still picking their bachelors. Isn't it exciting?"

"Definitely."

Before either of them could say more, another customer called Carol aside to show her one of Suzanna's clay figurines. Suzanna looked over everyone's heads to Jillian and smiled broadly. The opening was off to a great start. Nothing was going to ruin this day.

Chapter Five

T HIS WOULD BE no big deal.

So then why was he nervous?

Avery pulled his pickup to a stop a few spots down the street from Tangled Charms. He cut the engine and then rubbed his palms over his jeans. He assured himself his uneasiness was due to the fact he didn't have an alternate plan should Jillian reject the idea of mentoring him. It had nothing to do with seeing Jillian again.

Avery glanced out the pickup's window at Jillian's brand new shop. He recalled Jillian mentioning that she wanted to open her own shop someday. Avery just never expected it to happen so soon.

Was it wrong that he was a little bit envious of her? Beth had filled him in on how Jillian had risked it all by selling the house she'd bought with the money she'd inherited from her father. She'd moved into her mother's garage apartment in order to invest as much money as possible into this venture.

He was happy for her. He truly was, but it reminded him

of his own unattained dreams. By this point in his life, he'd planned to own his own place like the Crooked S Ranch on the outskirts of Marietta. And if he hadn't been a guardian for the past six years, his dream would be a reality.

Avery drew his thoughts up short, ashamed of himself for thinking such a thing. He loved his family with all of his heart. And he would do anything for them—hence his presence today at Tangled Charms.

With Jillian's help, he hoped to make a respectable showing at the Bake-Off. Jillian was so kind and patient. He'd witnessed her many times helping his brother and sister with their homework and showing them how to do basic cooking in the kitchen.

Jillian had always been a real lifesaver. But would she be willing to do it again? Was it even fair of him to ask her? He paused, not sure what to do. But then his phone buzzed with a new text message:

Beth: *Did you ask her?*

Avery: *I will.*

Beth: *Hurry up.*

Avery: *Stop pushing.*

Beth: *Let me know what she says.*

Avery climbed out of his pickup. His movements were slow and labored as his knee was not as mobile as he'd been hoping. Not all of the swelling had gone down. And the bruising was now dark and ugly. Today, he'd opted to wear the brace on the outside of his jeans. It was definitely not as comfortable. But he just couldn't bring himself to go about town in his sweats. And with the temperature below freezing, he couldn't wear shorts.

He greeted people he passed. A few stopped him to ask about his knee, but thanks to the weather, no one tarried too long.

At last, he arrived at the entrance to Tangled Charms. It had a fun yet elegant style. Wine, gold, and white colors adorned the outside of the store, from the front door to the sign hanging overhead. Clearly a lot of thought had gone into this place.

Once he stepped inside, his gaze was immediately drawn to the jewelry displays and all of the fantastic decorations. He knew he'd come to the right person. Jillian could take the plain and make it fancy. And that was exactly what he needed. He didn't need to just bake a cake. He had to make it stand out—in a good way.

Suzanna glanced up from where she was working behind the counter. "Well, look what the wind blew in. How are you doing, Avery?"

"Not too bad." He cleared his throat. "The shop looks really nice. I hope it goes well for you and Jillian."

"Thank you." Suzanna moved to the display case. "Did you stop by to pick out something for Beth?"

"No—"

"Oh, do you need a present for a special lady?"

He inwardly groaned. Why did everyone seem to think he had to be linked up with a woman to be happy? What was wrong with being a bachelor? For the first time in years, he could come and go as he pleased without worrying about a nanny. He was enjoying his alone time. At least that's what he kept telling himself when he'd catch himself talking to Marshmallow.

"Nope. No present needed. I actually came to speak with Jillian. Is she around?"

Suzanna's brows rose beneath her bangs. "Actually, she just stepped out. Can I give her a message?"

Just then the bell above the door rang out. Jillian stepped inside and stopped. Her gaze settled on him. "Avery, what's the matter?"

"Why does something have to be the matter?"

"Well, you're here. In my shop." And then a range of emotions flitted over her face. "Do you need something for your girlfriend?"

"Not you too. How come everyone in this town thinks I need to hook up with someone to be happy?"

Jillian held up her hand as though to fend off his barrage. "Hey, I didn't say that. I just don't understand why you would come here otherwise."

"I needed to talk to you." He glanced over his shoulder to find Suzanna hadn't moved. She was watching them with rapt interest. He turned to Jillian. "Can we go somewhere and talk?"

Jillian didn't say anything for a moment as though considering his request. "I'm sorry, but I'm working. We'll have to talk here. Is this about Romeo? Has he come to visit your house again?"

Avery shook his head. "No. Romeo hasn't returned, but Marshmallow hasn't been herself. I think she misses him."

"I didn't think they got along."

"I don't know." Avery rubbed the back of his neck. "Romeo was pretty persistent and each time he moved, she let him get a little closer. I think there may be something there."

"Oh boy, wait until my mother hears that her baby boy has a girlfriend."

"Her baby boy?"

Jillian nodded. "My mother treats that cat like he's human. And he is spoiled rotten. But you don't want to hear about any of that. What did you want to talk about?"

Avery shifted his weight to his good leg. "Beth called last night after you left."

Jillian's beautiful face creased with worry lines. "Is something the matter?"

"That depends on what you mean." He wasn't sure how to broach the subject.

"Avery, you're starting to worry me."

"Sorry. I promise Beth is healthy and her grades are good."

"Then what is it?"

"Have you heard about the fundraiser? You know, the one for Harry's House?"

Jillian nodded.

"It seems Beth and Joanie have put their heads together and decided I would be a good bachelor to enter in this baking competition."

"Oh." A small smile tugged at Jillian's glossy lips.

"This isn't funny. I know next to nothing about baking. And I prefer to keep it that way. That's what bakeries are for. But Beth has this idea in her head, and she thinks I can do anything."

"You do have to admit you bake the best cupcakes."

"Not you too." He glanced down at the white floor tiles. He lowered his voice. "I can't bake."

"But the cupcakes?"

He kept his voice low, not wanting his admission to become public knowledge. "I take my mother's recipe to the Copper Mountain bakery. Every year I pay them extra to make the cupcakes that Beth and Jordan have been receiving all their lives."

Jillian's mouth gaped. "And they never knew?"

He shook his head. "When they were younger, I made sure to mess up some dishes and make it seem like I'd been slaving away."

"But why?"

He shrugged. "I just didn't want them to think I didn't care enough to bake them myself. But I was so busy working at the Crooked S on top of rodeoing on the weekends—not to mention looking after them and the house—that I didn't have much free time. And the time I did have, I wanted to spend with them. So I took a shortcut. I guess it was wrong of me."

"I can't believe I didn't know this. After all of the years I was in and out of your house, there are still so many things I don't know about you. But your heart was in the right place. That's the important part."

"Really? You're not mad at me?"

"No. Why would I be? I think it's sweet that you went out of your way to make your brother and sister's birthdays special. And you kept your mother's memory alive."

"Thanks. But it has now gotten me into this mess. Beth thinks I can do this Bake-Off and I don't want to let her down."

"What do you plan to do?"

He shrugged. "I have to learn how to bake."

"Really?"

Did she have to sound so shocked that he'd attempt to bake? He swallowed his indignation. He hoped when he spoke that his voice didn't betray him.

"Can you help me? You know…teach me?"

WHOA!!!

Jillian had promised herself that she was done helping Avery Wainwright. He was a stubborn man who wanted to do things on his own. A man whose mere presence had devastating consequences to her common sense.

She needed to give him a polite no and walk away. But instead, she found herself standing there giving his request serious consideration. After all, it was for a good cause—

No. No. No.

She couldn't fall into old patterns, not even for Harry's House. "I'm sorry, but I can't. I've got this new business. I can't just skip out and leave Suzanna to manage everything on her own."

Over Avery's shoulder she saw Suzanna frowning at her and then signaling for her to go for it. What was up with Suzanna? Her friend knew that if she got involved with Avery again, it would just lead her to disappointment. He was only interested in one thing—the rodeo.

Avery's eyes pleaded with her. "Please, Jillian. I wouldn't ask you if it wasn't important."

Avery was begging her? She didn't know what to do about this. It felt kind of good having Avery plead with her. And with every second that he stared at her like that, her resistance was melting.

But would he think of her as anything other than some sort of tutor? She doubted it. If he hadn't noticed her before, he certainly wasn't going to notice her now.

Avery pressed his hands to his trim waist. "I know I'm

putting you in a tough spot, but I don't want to let everyone down. Beth says that Harry's family have already done the paperwork and put up the money to sponsor me."

"But how did they know you would be home for the Bake-Off?"

"This all happened while I was out of town. As soon as Beth found out about my accident, she phoned Joanie or something like that. I'm a little fuzzy on the details. You know Beth. She talks quickly and skims over details. Anyway, I'm not sure how it all worked out, but I'm officially signed up now."

"Jillian, you don't have to worry about the shop," Suzanna chimed in with a big smile. "I've got it."

Both Suzanna and Avery looked at Jillian with expectant gazes.

"I...I don't know." Warring emotions raged within her—common sense versus compassion. "I'll need to think about it."

"Oh." There was definitely a dejected tone in his voice. "I understand."

Guilt ensued. She stifled it. Why should she always be waiting in the wings when he needed something? Any other time, he didn't have time for her.

"I'll let you know," she said.

"She'll have an answer for you tomorrow," Suzanna said and then grinned like a Cheshire cat.

When Avery turned to thank Suzanna for being so understanding, Jillian glared at her best friend. How could she side against her? Suzanna knew about their history and how the whole town was certain after playing house all of those years that she and Avery would eventually marry. But when the kids no longer needed her, she realized that neither did Avery.

He turned back to Jillian. "Thanks. I appreciate you considering it. I know you've already done so much for me and my family."

When he was gone, Jillian turned on Suzanna. "What were you doing?"

"Helping you out."

"No, you weren't. You were just making things worse."

Suzanna sent her a look of disbelief. "And how do you get that?"

"Because you know I swore off that man."

"What I know is that no other man can live up to the image of Avery that you have stuck in your mind."

"That's not true." Was it? No, of course not. "I've been out there dating."

"Exactly. None of them have stuck around. You broke up with them for one reason or another."

"That's not true." And then she realized that in part it was true. "Glenn was the one who dumped me."

"And he was a fool."

"Now that's something I can agree with you on."

"So what are you going to do about Avery?"

"If I was smart, I'd give him a polite but firm no."

"But it's for a good cause and the whole town is counting on him making a respectable showing."

Jillian groaned. "Stop. I don't need you pressuring me."

"That's because you already know you want to help him. It's in your nature. You always help everyone. Look at me."

"What about you?"

Suzanna rolled her eyes. "Don't go acting all innocent. You knew I really wanted to go into business with you, but I couldn't come up with half of the investment so you sold your house to make our dream come true. And I will never be able to repay you—"

"Stop." Heat rushed to Jillian's face. She hadn't done anything that Suzanna wouldn't have done if the roles had been reversed. "You did me the favor, because I never would have been able to pull this shop off on my own."

Suzanna busied herself wiping the fingerprints from one of the glass cases. "So as I was saying, you know you will help him. The only question is how long will you hold out until you admit it to yourself?"

Jillian didn't know. But it wasn't going to be today. She at least had enough self-respect not to cave as soon as Avery asked.

Chapter Six

T HE FOLLOWING MORNING, Jillian placed a coffee cup in the dishwasher. It was her usual Tuesday breakfast at her mother's house. She wasn't sure how the tradition had started, but they'd been doing it for years now. They were both so busy that this weekly breakfast was the one time they could catch up over coffee, eggs, and bagels. Jillian's diet always took a hit, but she knew how much her mother looked forward to the time together.

"Did you get it yet?"

Jillian straightened and turned to her mother. She had absolutely no idea what her mother was talking about. She could only assume she'd forgotten something for the shop's grand opening week. She just hoped whatever it was that it wasn't too late to rectify. "Did I get what?"

"Your dress."

"Dress?" She wasn't wearing a dress to work, not even for the grand opening of Tangled Charms.

Her mother nodded. "You know, for the wedding." When Jillian continued to send her mother a puzzled look, her mother added, "Surely you didn't forget your cousin's wedding? It's this weekend."

"Oh." Truthfully, she had forgotten about it. She told herself it was all of the last-minute details for the grand opening that had her distracted, but if she was honest with herself, she didn't want to think about the wedding.

Everyone she knew seemed to be getting married or having babies. And then there was her. The one big disappointment to her mother. She had no man in her life. And no chance of giving her mother a grandbaby. She didn't even have so much as a dog, cat, or goldfish. There was just her. And her mother routinely fussed over her bare ring finger.

Her mother ran the dishcloth over the table. "I take it by your response that you forgot about the wedding."

"Something like that."

"I figured that would happen so I RSVP'd for you. And I included a plus one for you."

"But I don't have anyone to go with me."

"You could always ask Glenn."

"We broke up."

Her mother frowned. "I know you did. But why? He seemed so nice."

"I don't want to talk about it." It didn't matter what she said, it wouldn't erase her mother's disappointment. "I can just go by myself—"

"No. That won't work. We don't want you going all by

yourself when all of your friends will be with their significant others. I'll check and see if one of my friends' single sons will escort you—"

"No. Don't."

Her mother arched a perfectly plucked brow. "Does that mean you have someone special in mind?"

Panic jumbled her thoughts. She just couldn't have her mother planning out her love life. Once her mother started, she wouldn't stop. So far, Jillian had managed on her own. "Yes, I do."

The worry lines etching her mother's face smoothed. "That's wonderful. Who is it?"

"I'm not telling you because I haven't asked him yet." She didn't even know who the 'him' would be.

Her mother's whole demeanor became more amenable. "You check with your friend and see if he's available. I'll need to know as soon as possible. If your idea doesn't work, I'll call my friends." Her mother glanced at the clock. "Well, I better get moving. I don't want to be late for work."

Jillian hustled out the door. She was in serious trouble. If she didn't come up with her own date, her mother would take it upon herself to make sure she had an escort. It was her mother's mission to make sure Jillian had a happy, fulfilled life like she'd had with Jillian's father until a massive heart attack stole him away.

Jillian didn't have a clue where she'd find a date for the wedding, but there had to be some guy around Marietta who wouldn't mind some free food and dancing. Right?

It had warmed up since yesterday, melting the snow. Jillian decided it was a good day to walk to work. She was surprised to find how many Marietta residents were out and about. She smiled and waved hello to everyone she passed. She inquired about the health of some and thanked others for their kind words about Tangled Charms.

She also passed some of Marietta's good-looking men. There was Cormac Sheehan. Definitely a fine-looking man, but taken. And then she passed by Jasper Flint, another Marietta man who was off the market. Where were all of the single guys this morning?

Probably hiding because they'd heard that her mother was out to set her up on a date. Jillian couldn't blame them. In her experience, being set up on a date was the worst. There had to be one man who was gallant enough to ride to her rescue. But who?

By the time Jillian entered the shop, she was frowning. She hadn't thought of any candidates. All she'd succeeded in doing was giving herself a headache.

"Good morning." Suzanna's face lit up with a smile.

"Morning." Jillian rubbed her forehead.

"Whoa. What's wrong with you?"

"My mother."

"What has she done now?"

Jillian held up a finger to get Suzanna to wait. She headed straight for the coffee pot and poured herself a cup. Then she rummaged around in her purse until she found a bottle of painkillers. She popped a couple aspirin in her mouth and swallowed them down with coffee. She choked, realizing that she'd forgotten the milk and sweetener.

Her mind was scattered. As the years passed by, her mother was getting more assertive about finding Jillian a husband. She didn't actually say husband, but Jillian knew it was her mother's ultimate goal.

"Are you okay?" Suzanna sent her a concerned look.

"Just forgot the sweetener." Jillian checked to make sure they were alone. "My mother is trying to set me up, again."

Suzanna got a big grin on her face.

"This isn't funny," Jillian ground out.

Suzanna struggled to maintain a straight face, but the amusement reflected in her green eyes. "And who's the lucky guy?"

"I don't think she cares as long as I have a date in time for my cousin's wedding."

"Oh. I see." Suzanna turned the closed sign in the window to open.

"Why are you so amused by all of this? If your mother were to do this to you, I don't think you'd be amused at all."

"True. But thankfully my mother is remarried and living in Seattle. I think I'm pretty safe from her meddling." Suzanna moved behind the jewelry counter and started to switch on all of the display lights. "What are you going to do?"

"I don't know. Would you believe my mother has me so worried over what she might do that I evaluated every man I passed on the way to work for their dating qualifications."

"And did you find any potential dates?"

"No. They were either too old or too young or too married."

"What about Avery—"

"No!" Jillian glowered at her best friend.

"But—"

"Suzanna, you of all people know that he's completely off limits to me."

"Listen, I know he hurt you, but I thought you said you were past it."

"I am. That's why I don't want to ask him on a date."

"Who said it has to be a real date? Couldn't it just be two friends hanging out together?"

"Really?" Jillian sent her a disbelieving look. "At a wedding, with my mother and the rest of my family? How's that going to work?"

Suzanna shrugged. "Well, I'm out of ideas. Let me know who you come up with."

This was just great. Not even her best friend could think of a respectable date for her. Because she was never ever going to walk up to Avery and ask him to be her plus one to this wedding. There had to be a better solution. She just had to give it some more thought.

HE WAS BORED.

How was that possible?

Not so long ago, there weren't enough hours in the day for everything he needed to accomplish. Now the house was empty, but his knee refused to cooperate so that he could work at the Crooked S. Other than physical therapy a few mornings a week, he had absolutely no pressing matters. For the first time in forever, he could do as he pleased.

Avery stared at the kitchen wall where he'd just finished removing the ivory tile backsplash that had been there all of his life. It was in desperate need of updating. In fact, the whole kitchen needed updating, including the floor.

He wasn't supposed to be standing on his leg for long stretches, but he at least wanted to get the backsplash installed. When he'd been home previously, he'd painted the walls from a sunny yellow to a muted mossy green with white trim. The new stainless steel appliances were ordered. It'd taken him nearly a year now, but soon the whole house would be remodeled.

The thought of selling the house had crossed his mind, but just as quickly, he dismissed it. The house was the last tangible connection to his parents. And as he'd already played a part in his parents' death, he wouldn't take anything else from his siblings. After fixing the house up, he could wash his hands of it and hand it over to his sister.

"Murr…" Marshmallow strolled into the kitchen. She sat down next to the kitchen table and let out a big yawn.

Avery smiled and shook his head. "It looks like you had a rough day."

She walked over to him and rubbed against his legs. He bent over and scratched behind her ear. "Is this your way of letting me know it's dinnertime?"

She glanced up at him and murred.

Avery checked the clock to find out that it was well past dinnertime. He grabbed a tin of cat food from under the counter. In no time, Marshmallow was devouring her meal.

Just then his phone rang. His first thought was that it was Jillian. At last, she'd decided to give him an answer. He knew he'd just asked her the day before, but if she wouldn't help him, he had to find someone who would mentor him. So far, he hadn't come up with any possibilities.

He pressed a button on his phone. Before he could get a word out, he heard Beth say, "Did you ask her?"

No hello or any other sort of greeting from his sister. It was typical for him to feel as though he'd just stepped into the middle of a conversation when Beth got excited about something.

Ever since his younger sister went off to college, she made it a point to keep tabs on him. It was as though their roles had been reversed. And then there was his brother who took off for the military and rarely phoned home.

Avery knew what his sister was asking—if he'd talked to

Jillian about the Bake-Off. He hesitated, not liking being pushed.

"Avery?" Beth's tone held a note of impatience. "You did ask Jillian to help you, didn't you?"

He inhaled a deep breath and counted to five before he answered. "I did."

"And?"

Marshmallow finished eating and jumped up on the table. She wasn't allowed up there, but just like Beth, the cat didn't listen to him all that often. The cat head-butted his hand until he started to pet her. And then a loud purr emanated from her.

He turned his attention back to the other insistent female in his life. "Did anyone ever accuse you of being pushy?"

"Yes. You. Now spill. What did she say?"

"Nothing." He hadn't heard a word from Jillian since he'd asked her to help him. He took the silence as her answer. She'd done enough for his family and she didn't want to do any more.

"What do you mean nothing? She had to say something."

He raked his fingers through his hair. "Beth, would you quit pushing this? Besides, I'm the big brother; I'm the one who is supposed to be asking the questions. So how are classes going?"

"Don't change the subject. What did Jillian say?"

He might as well answer her, because he knew Beth wouldn't let up until he did. "She said she needed to think about it."

"And when was this?"

"Really? You're going to keep grilling me?"

"Yes," Beth said matter-of-factly. "When did you speak to her?"

"Yesterday. Now I'm done answering your questions," he grouched. At that point, Marshmallow decided to make a quick exit. Perhaps his voice had been a bit harsh. He made a point of speaking in a less hostile tone. "Don't you have a test to study for or some such thing?"

"Actually, I just finished. I'm walking back to my dorm room from the library." She paused as though she'd just thought of something.

Avery inwardly groaned. It'd been a long day and he just wasn't up for more. "I should let you go—"

"I could speak to Jillian for you. You know, put in a good word—"

"No." When he didn't hear a response, he said, "Beth, don't you dare interfere. You do realize that I'm an adult, right?"

"But I also know you're not so good with the women—"

"Hey! We aren't talking about my dating life. I only asked Jillian to teach me to bake. That is all. And don't you dare go and get any ideas. I have too much going on in my life. I don't want a girlfriend."

"You always have an excuse not to get serious with any-one. Before it was because you had Jordan and me to raise. But now we're out on our own. You don't have any more excuses."

"Beth…"

"If you don't ask Jillian again, I will." There was a slight pause. "Or better yet, I'll drive home and teach you myself."

"No. You have school."

"I can make arrangements."

"No." When she didn't say anything, he worried that she'd totally ignored him and was already hatching some plan that would involve her missing classes. There was only one way to stop her and she probably knew it. Still, the responsible part of him forced him to sacrifice his pride for his sister's welfare. "You don't need to come home. I will speak to Jillian again."

"Good." There was a muffled sound and then the mur-mur of voices. "Hey, Avery, I've got to go."

After they disconnected the call, he shook his head. His little sister knew exactly how to manipulate him and he fell for it every time. Still, the thought of speaking to Jillian again wasn't as bad as he was making it out to be. He enjoyed her company and he found her absence around the house was quite noticeable.

Chapter Seven

T WO DAYS.

That's how long Jillian had been holding out without giving Avery an answer. She figured that since the competition didn't start for another couple of weeks, she had a little time before she had to give him a firm answer.

And she'd been busy. She'd found out through Carol Bingley that Jane McCullough was helping the Chamber of Commerce organize the fundraiser. After a couple of phone calls, Jillian had learned that there would be a craft sale during the first round of the Bake-Off at the local high school.

Jillian ran her ideas past Jane and got two thumbs up. Now she just had to keep moving in order to get everything arranged in time for the big event. And the first part was just about complete.

Jillian scanned the computer monitor to make sure she hadn't missed anything with the order of rubber wristbands in a wide assortment of colors. Her finger hovered over the place-order button as she inspected the design one last time.

The design couldn't be girly or else none of the male population would consider wearing them. So she'd gone with: Harry's House. To the left of the text was the black silhouette of a house and on the right was the black silhouette of a saw and hammer crossed over one another. The wristbands were neutral and hopefully would catch on with all of the town's residents. All proceeds would go to the Harry's House fund.

She clicked on the order button.

And now that left the question of helping Avery—

"Nice place," called out a familiar male voice.

Jillian glanced up from where she was sitting behind the counter. Her gaze focused on Glenn. Surely he wouldn't have the audacity to show his face here. She blinked, but he was still there.

"I see I caught you off guard." He smiled, flashing his brilliant white teeth.

That was the same smile that at one time had made her stomach dip like she was on a tall roller coaster. But no more. She was inoculated against his charms.

"Hello, Glenn." She kept her voice even, refusing to let him evoke any further noticeable reaction in her.

He removed his dark sunglasses and slid them into the pocket of his black leather coat. He liked to dress up like he was some movie star instead of a small-time actor who did local commercials for grocery and hardware stores.

He sauntered over to the counter and leaned an elbow on

it. "I know you missed me."

Jillian almost gagged. Was he serious? Not an apology but rather an accusation.

"What do you want, Glenn?"

His tone grew softer and more cajoling. "I want to talk to you."

Hadn't he gotten the hint that she didn't want to talk to him when she never picked up his calls and failed to return his voicemails? Then again, Glenn was always all about Glenn, and he didn't understand that others might not like him as much as he liked himself. What had she ever seen in him? It totally escaped her now.

Jillian closed her laptop. "We don't have anything to discuss."

"Yes, we do." He sighed. "I'm sorry. All right?"

He thought that was going to make up for dumping her in public? They'd been dining at the time. Luckily, it had been in Bozeman. Yet, the restaurant had been packed and Glenn hadn't been discreet.

He'd wanted her to drop everything to go on a promotional shoot with him. He'd told her in no uncertain terms that he was tired of coming in a distant second to her outlandish dreams of being a business owner. At least now he could see Tangled Charms with his own eyes—see that she'd succeeded as a business owner.

"Is there something I can show you?" she asked, pretending he was nothing more than a customer—a less than welcome customer.

"What?" It took him a second to figure out what she was up to. "Come on, Jilly. Won't you give me a chance? I'm here after all. And I know you need a date."

"You what?"

"I ran into your mother. She mentioned something about you being invited to a wedding."

"And she asked you to take me?" Please say it wasn't so. Surely her own mother wouldn't turn against her. Would she?

"No. She didn't ask. But I can take a hint."

Take a hint? Or make up an excuse to see her? Jillian really wanted to believe that he took advantage of her mother's ramblings in order to insinuate himself back into her life.

At that point, the door chimed. Suzanna returned from her dentist appointment. And right behind her were a couple of ladies who were good friends with Carol Bingley. Which meant everything that was said between her and Glenn would become the subject of town gossip. And that was the very last thing Jillian needed right now. When people spoke of her, she wanted them taking her seriously and talking highly of her business pursuit. She did not want them talking about how she'd been dumped by this movie-star-wannabe.

"Come on, Jilly. Have some coffee with me? We can discuss this wedding." Glenn looked at her as though she couldn't possibly turn down such an offer.

It was so tempting to tell him exactly what he could do

with his offer, but she glanced at the two older ladies who were not even trying to hide the fact they were eavesdropping. Jillian inwardly groaned. Why were so many people interested in her social life?

It'd be the same way at the wedding. She imagined all of the pitying looks from her married relatives—the same looks she'd received at a prior wedding. Seriously, didn't they hear that this was a new age where women didn't have to marry by the age of eighteen? She wasn't an old maid. She just hadn't found the right guy and she was starting to think that her Mr. Right didn't exist.

And then she realized that instead of fighting Glenn's advances maybe she should take a different approach. She could go out with him one more time—to the wedding. It might not be the sort of date he was hoping for and it might end abruptly, but he owed her.

By having Glenn escort her to the wedding, she'd be putting off the inevitable. Somehow that didn't sound so bad. But could she really spend an entire evening with him in such a romantic setting?

She turned to Suzanna, who'd just stepped out of the office. "Could you handle the shop for a few minutes?"

Suzanna didn't smile. Her gaze moved from Jillian to Glenn and then back again. Jillian knew Suzanna didn't like Glenn, but she was too much of a lady to tell him to his face what she really thought of him.

Jillian, wanting to speak to Glenn in private, glanced

back at Suzanna and then nodded over her shoulder at their audience. The light of dawning flashed in Suzanna's eyes.

"Sure. I've got it." Suzanna moved to greet their customers.

Jillian rushed to grab her coat. Luckily, the Java Café was just a couple of doors down. She'd get a to-go cup and be out of there in a couple of minutes. Just long enough for her to address the idea of going to the wedding together.

HAVE PATIENCE.

That's what the doctor had told Avery when he'd gone in for a checkup. The swelling in his knee was decreasing and the bruising was starting to fade to a greenish color. Avery wanted to hear that he'd make a miraculous recovery, but the doctor said it would take time.

Avery checked his phone for the tenth time that morning. Still no missed calls and no text messages.

Have patience. The doctor's words echoed in his mind. It appeared that advice applied to a number of facets of Avery's life.

But why hadn't Jillian called? It wasn't like her to be forgetful. She was always on top of everything. For a long time, she'd helped keep his life organized.

But now she had Tangled Charms. And it was the opening week. That was it; she'd gotten distracted. Or she was tired of bailing him out. She had been such a good sport over the years—always there to pick up the pieces.

Avery eased his pickup through town, not sure what to do. He definitely couldn't do this Bachelor Bake-Off without her guidance. Would it be so bad if he were to stop by Tangled Charms?

Deciding a reminder was the best course of action, he turned onto Main Street. He'd stop by and clear this up in no time.

As he was nearing the Java Café, he spotted Jillian. He slowed down, hoping to gain her attention. And then he noticed she wasn't alone. There was a man with her—someone Avery didn't recognize. The man was much taller than Jillian and he was well dressed.

They were laughing. It was obvious even from this distance that they were quite familiar with each other. Avery's fingers tightened on the steering wheel. He wondered if this was the reason for Jillian's distraction.

And then the man stepped in front of Jillian and without preamble he leaned forward to kiss her.

Avery's gut knotted up. He'd seen enough. He turned his gaze away and tramped on the gas a little harder, not wanting to witness any more of Jillian's life. If that's what she wanted, who was he to complain?

But what did he do now?

Let his sister and the town down by backing out of the event?

Or give this baking thing a try on his own? After all, how hard could it be?

OH NO! NO! NO!

This can't be happening.

Jillian jumped back before Glenn's lips touched hers. She stared up at him. "What are you doing?"

A frown wiped away his smile. "As if you didn't know. I was trying to kiss you." He arched a brow. "What are you doing? Trying to play hard to get?"

She wasn't playing. She had absolutely no interest in him kissing her. Not now. Not ever again. What had she been thinking to even consider him as her escort to the wedding? She would go alone before she would ask him.

She leveled her shoulders and lifted her chin. "Glenn, I think we need to get something straight. I'm not interested in you. Not now. Not in the future."

For a moment, his mouth gaped. And then he pressed his lips together into a firm line. A tense moment passed. "Enough with this game. I know you weren't happy about how we ended things, but what choice did I have? You were never around. You were always here in Marietta with that hobby of yours."

"That hobby you're referring to is my business. A successful one that has expanded from the internet to a physical store." She refused to let anyone demean her efforts.

"And now that you've gotten it out of your system, I figured you'd come to your senses. That's why I'm here—to give you another chance."

Was he serious? The sincere look on his face said that he was. The ego on this guy had no bounds.

"This conversation is over. We are over. Goodbye, Glenn." She turned and strode down the sidewalk.

"You'll regret this," he called out to her back. "I don't know what I ever saw in you. You just used me to get exposure for that hobby of yours. I was just a leg up for you. You only care about yourself."

He was so wrong about her. She did care about others. Just not him.

She didn't slow down. She kept going. All the while, she hoped that not many people heard his parting words. How dare he shout out those lies?

And then Avery's face came to mind. She'd never answered him. Was she being selfish about her time? Was that why she was holding back?

Anxious to prove Glenn wrong and assure herself that she hadn't changed, she pulled her phone out. She selected Avery's phone number.

It rang once before he answered. "Hello."

"Hey, Avery, I was wondering if you wanted to get together to go over your game plan for the Bake-Off." There was a pause as though she'd surprised him with the offer. "Avery? Are you still there?"

"Yes. But listen, I understand that you don't have time. It's okay—"

"If I didn't have time, I'd have said so." It was true. She wasn't afraid to speak up. The problem was when she was torn in two different directions. And that happened frequently where Avery was concerned. "So what about this evening?"

There was a pause as though he was considering it. "I have plans."

"Oh. Well, we can do it another time."

"I don't think so. Sorry I bothered you. Goodbye."

The line went dead. She stared at the phone wondering what had just happened. He was the one who had just asked her a couple of days ago to help him out. And now he was dismissing her without any explanation.

"Whatever," she muttered to herself as she pulled open the door to Tangled Charms. She obviously did not understand men at all.

When she stepped in the shop, she was pleased to find a few people making their way around the various display cases. And these people were not friends of her mother. They were passersby and hopefully future customers. At least this part of her life was looking up.

Jillian rushed to the office to deposit her coat. She told herself she should be relieved. This way there was no possibility that she'd get sucked back into Avery's world. Not that she was vulnerable to his charming smile. Once upon a time, she may have had the craziest crush on him, but that was long over. She'd learned how to stand her ground.

Still, she found it odd that Avery would back out of such a good cause. After all, it was in memory of a friend. And it would benefit the community. And then she realized that she must have waited too long to give him an answer. He'd no doubt found someone else to help him.

She'd just hung up her coat and turned around to find Suzanna standing in the doorway of the office. Startled, Jillian said, "I didn't hear you follow me."

With a serious expression, Suzanna arched a brow. "So? Did you really sink low enough to accept his too-little-too-late apology?"

"Wait. You thought I was going to get back together with Glenn?"

Suzanna shrugged, looking a bit worried. "Please say you're not taking him back."

"I'm not. Definitely not. I was considering asking him to be my escort to the wedding, but I just couldn't do it." She shook her head as she headed back to the showroom. "There's not a chance. I don't know what I ever saw in him."

Suzanna trailed behind her. "What a relief." Suzanna audibly sighed as she sunk down on a stool behind the jewelry counter. "What are you going to do about the wedding?"

Just then Dan walked in the door. He was their handyman, who'd helped turn their dream into reality. He knew a little bit of everything from electrical work to carpentry and plumbing. His father was a handyman and had taught him the tricks of the trade.

"Hi, ladies." When Dan smiled, the dimples in his cheeks showed.

"Hi." Both Jillian and Suzanna said in unison.

He brushed his blond hair back off his face. "I have the new light fixture for the office. If you don't mind, I can put it up now."

"No problem," Suzanna said. "My eyes will be so grateful for the brighter lighting."

With his toolbox in one hand and the cardboard box with the new light fixture under the other arm, he made his way back to the office. Jillian moved to the worktable she'd set up behind the jewelry counter so she could work and keep an eye on the store.

Suzanna rushed over to her. "What about him?"

"What about who?"

"Dan. You know." She waggled her brows like Jillian was supposed to follow her train of thought.

"Suzanna, whatever it is just say it—"

"Shh…" Suzanna glanced over her shoulder as though to make sure they weren't overheard. "What about asking Dan to the wedding?"

"Seriously?" The thought never even crossed her mind. He was a few years younger than her and they had nothing in common. And it would just be weird since he was their handyman. "I can't."

"Sure you can."

"But he sort of works for us."

"Not after he puts in that new light. He'll be all done." Suzanna gave her a little push. "Go ask him."

"Suzanna!"

"Shh... Just go do it. What do you have to lose? After all, you almost asked Glenn. Dan is quite a few steps up from him. And he's very easy on the eyes."

Was she really that pathetic that she would ask just about anyone to go with her? Yes. It was better than one of her mother's friends' sons. Jillian had been down that road more than once and it was difficult. And knowing that her mother would most likely get a report back on the date made it that much more awkward.

"Fine," Jillian whispered. She strolled back to the office where Dan was up on the ladder. "How's it going?"

"Good. Hey, would you mind handing me that smaller Phillips head screwdriver in the top of my toolbox?"

Jillian fished around until she found the right tool and handed it up to him. She couldn't believe what she was about to do. Still, the thought of what she'd endure showing up at her cousin's wedding alone or with one of her mother's blind dates spurred her on.

She swallowed hard. "Hey, Dan, what are you doing this weekend?"

He paused from loosening a screw to look at her. "Aw, don't tell me you have another project for me that needs to be done ASAP."

"Well, not exactly—"

"Oh, good. Then it can wait until next week."

"No, it can't." Her palms grew moist and her mouth dry. "I wanted to see if you'd go to a wedding with me on Saturday."

His screwdriver slipped. The tip broke the old light fixture. Dan jerked back, almost falling off the ladder. Not exactly the reaction she'd been expecting.

"Sorry about that." He looked a bit flustered as he examined the damage.

"Don't worry. We didn't want to keep it."

"I can pay you."

She shook her head. "It was my fault for talking to you while you were working." Distracted by the accident, Dan seemed to have forgotten the question. Jillian swallowed hard. "So what do you say?"

He didn't look at her. "About what?"

She fidgeted with the hem on her blouse. "Going to the wedding."

He stepped down off the ladder. "Oh. Um…I don't know how to tell you this."

Was it just her imagination or had his chest puffed up? And had he suddenly got a bit taller? Jillian rushed to smooth things. "It's okay if you're busy."

His demeanor had gone from flustered to something much calmer. "I didn't know you felt that way about me. I wish I had."

Felt what way? He thought she had a thing for him? Ugh! This was a disaster.

"You don't understand—"

"I think I do." He fidgeted with the screwdriver. "I hate to let you down, but I have a girlfriend. And we have plans this weekend."

Since when did Dan have a girlfriend? How had she missed that? Boy, she was making a mess out of everything today. She wondered what else she'd been missing.

Her face was so hot now that an egg could be fried on it. "I'm sorry. I...I didn't know about your girlfriend. Just forget I said anything."

She whirled around and fled the office. She rushed out to the showroom so fast that Suzanna got a startled look on her face. She excused herself from a customer and came over to Jillian.

"What's the matter?"

Jillian didn't know whether to be angry with herself for making a fool of herself or if she should be embarrassed for trolling for a date.

"I...I asked Dan if he'd go to the wedding with me."

"And..."

"I made an utter fool of myself."

"Why? What happened?"

Jillian's face was still hot. "He has a girlfriend."

"He does?"

"And it gets worse. Now he thinks I have the hots for him. This is a fine mess." She wanted to lay the blame at her mother's feet, but she couldn't. She'd been just as eager to save face in front of her cousins and family as her mother had been. "Since when did having a significant other become so vital? I'm fine on my own."

Suzanna arched a brow. "Does that mean I don't have to worry about you asking out more men who are otherwise off the market?"

Jillian glared at her best friend. "I'm done. I'm going to the wedding alone."

Chapter Eight

THIS DAY HAD taken a very sudden and very strange turn. Avery climbed out of his pickup and made his way up the steps of the sprawling log house at the Crooked S Ranch. The air was crisp but the sun's rays held the promise of warmth. Being here was bittersweet now that Howard Smith had passed on.

Avery paused on the porch that spanned the front of the house. He gazed up at the front of the house. It was a wall of windows that looked out over the sprawling pasture. And when the sun rose in the morning, it was truly magnificent.

He moved to the wood rail that ran the length of the porch. Avery brushed off the snow and braced his hands on the cold log rail. His gaze stretched out over the hundreds of acres. He'd always loved this view. It was the most beautiful sight in the world—except for Jillian.

Wait. Where had that thought come from?

He gave himself a mental shake and focused on the here and now. He just couldn't believe that as of this morning, he had been presented with an opportunity to own this gorgeous ranch. But with his depleted savings and his diminishing number of product endorsements, he'd need a miracle to make this dream a reality.

The sound of boots on the steps drew Avery's attention back to the present. He turned to find his good friend Blake Ridgeway, foreman of the Crooked S, approaching him.

"I didn't think you were supposed to be back in town for a while," Blake said, coming to a stop next to him.

"My knee had other ideas."

Blake's gaze dipped to the knee brace. "I see. How is it?"

"Good enough that I don't have to have surgery, but not good enough for me to return to the rodeo circuit. The doc doesn't want me riding horses for a while."

"That's too bad. You were off to a good start."

Avery tilted his cowboy hat up on his forehead. "Doesn't it always work that way?"

"Normally I'd tell you to saddle up because we could use the help rotating the cattle to the south field, but seeing your leg isn't up for it, I guess we'll have to muddle through without you."

Avery shrugged. "When have I ever let a little scrape stop me? I'll help out."

"No, you won't." Blake was a few years older than Avery and the more cautious of the two of them. "I'm sorry I mentioned it."

Avery wasn't up for arguing the point. He was still a bit dazed by all that had happened since he woke up that morning. It had all started with a knock on the door.

He'd been working the kitchen remodel when the postman had arrived with a certified letter. Avery had to admit that he'd been hesitant about signing his name and accepting the mysterious piece of mail. The last time he'd accepted certified mail, it had been after his parents' deaths. Those had been the papers regarding the custody of his brother and sister.

He'd hoped and prayed this current piece of mail didn't come with such staggering consequences. Still, he had no idea what it might be. And then to find the name of a law firm as the return address, he was certain his life was about to take a turn. But he had no idea at the time if it'd be for the better or worse.

However, when he ripped the envelope open, he'd received the surprise of his life. Howard Smith, the owner of the Crooked S, had written into his will that Avery was to be granted an exclusive opportunity to buy the ranch. The letter went on to say that the ranch had undergone a full evaluation and that the specified dollar figure represented the ranch's current value. It also stated that he had ninety days in order to secure the necessary funds or else the ranch would be put up for public auction. The proceeds were to be split evenly between Howard's two nephews.

After filling Blake in on the recent events, Avery turned back to the most amazing view. "I knew Howard always talked about wanting someone who loved the land and animals as much as him to one day own the place, but I never thought he meant me."

"He thought of you like a son. You were here for years before I came along. You worked every day from sunup until sundown. I remember how upset your mother would get because you were never home."

"But my father understood. He loved when his work brought him to this ranch, even if he only did the accounting and bookwork. I think if he hadn't had a family counting on him to provide for them, he would have chucked the accounting and become a cowboy."

"Sounds like a good plan to me. I couldn't imagine doing anything else with my life."

"Me either."

Blake studied him for a moment. "So when are you going to buy the place? I know all of the ranch hands will be happy to have you running the Crooked S."

"Whoa! Slow down. Before that can happen, I need to devise a plan to come up with the funds to pay the hefty price tag. I knew owning two thousand acres of this rich fertile land wouldn't be cheap, but I wasn't quite prepared for such a staggering asking price."

"But don't forget that includes three hundred head of cattle. Plus all of the outbuildings. Not to mention this beautiful home that's just begging for a family to move in and fill it with smiles and laughter."

Avery stepped back and waved off his friend. "What's up

with the hard sale line?"

Blake glanced down. "There are a lot of lives hinging on your decision. I just had to talk my best man out of leaving today. Everyone thinks the ranch will be sold off and chunked up into smaller ranches or that the new owner will bring in their own people."

Just what Avery needed, more pressure to make this happen. And it might have been a possibility, if he hadn't gotten injured. He'd been at the top of his division. There were advertisers vying for his signature, but after his injury he hadn't heard a peep out of them.

"Sorry," Blake said. "I shouldn't have laid all of that on you. It's just that I get so frustrated. I know this ranch can be successful again instead of scraping by. It just needs someone young and ambitious."

Avery let out a laugh and it felt good. "And you think I'm that person?"

"Sure. And I'm not the only one."

"What's that supposed to mean?"

"Do you honestly think Mr. Smith would have named you in his will if he didn't trust you with one of the great loves of his life?"

Avery turned his back on the ranch. The pressure to come up with the necessary funds to help out the ranch hands at the Crooked S and live up to Howard's expectations was a lot for him. Just for now, he needed to think about something else.

"Have you heard about that Bachelor Bake-Off?" Avery asked, hoping to change the subject.

"Who hasn't heard about it? It's all folks are talking about in Marietta."

"And what do you think of the idea?" He wanted to get a guy's perspective on it before he decided what to do about staying in the competition or backing out.

"I think it's a bit different. But it's for a good cause. Harry was a great guy. He'd like the town pulling together."

"You think so?"

"I think he'd get a kick out of a bunch of guys getting up in front of the whole town and baking, especially the ones who aren't exactly experienced." Blake paused and arched a brow. "Why are you so interested?"

Avery swallowed. "I'm one of the bachelors."

"You are? How did that happen?" But before Avery could answer, Blake said, "Never mind. I know. It was Beth."

"Good guess."

"It was easy. Seems that girl has been getting you involved in all sorts of interesting things, from father-daughter dances to chaperoning field trips. Well, you can count on me to cheer you on. I just have one question. Do you know how to bake?"

"I think I'll plead the fifth."

Blake whistled. "Oh boy are you in trouble."

"Don't I know it."

His only hope had been Jillian. And now he didn't know what to do. He had to do something before Beth heard and came rushing home. He didn't need to be the cause of his little sister failing out of school.

His thoughts strayed to Jillian. When had she gained a boyfriend? She'd been so caught up in her business and settling into her mother's garage apartment that he didn't think she'd take time out for a relationship. Obviously, he'd been wrong.

The memory of her about to kiss another man left a bitter taste in Avery's mouth. He assured himself that it wasn't jealousy. He was just going to miss her assistance. That was all.

THE ONE GOOD thing about living next door to your parent was being able to borrow things.

Jillian sat at her mother's kitchen table with a stack of cookbooks in front of her. Suzanna had agreed that they should keep up the coffee and pastries at the shop for a week or two longer. Jillian wanted to switch up what they offered so she was hunting for ideas—and trying not to wonder about Avery's sudden change of mind about her helping him.

"Oh, hi," her mother said as she entered through the back door.

Her mother's arms were full of groceries. Jillian jumped to her feet to help. Once the bags were on the table, Jillian asked if there were more in the car.

"No. This is it, but thank you." Her mother slipped off her coat and hung it over the back of a chair. "What are you up to?"

"I was just looking through your cookbooks." She'd found a couple of intriguing recipes, but she couldn't decide which to bake. "Do you mind if I borrow a few?"

"Not at all. Maybe if you tell me what you're planning to bake, I could help you find a recipe."

"See that's the thing, I have no idea what I want to bake."

Her mother straightened from switching into her slippers. "Is this for a special occasion? Perhaps for Glenn?"

She wished her mother would stop bringing up his name. Jillian had avoided the details of her breakup with Glenn because, well, they were embarrassing. She didn't know what bothered her more—the fact she'd fallen for such a superficial person in the first place or that she'd been dumped in public. But she supposed it was best to clear the air.

"Mom, Glenn dumped me. And I'm never taking him back."

"He did? Why didn't you ever say anything?"

"Because it's embarrassing and I just didn't want to talk about it."

"Oh, sweetie, you should have said something a long

time ago. Here I was going on and on. I feel so bad now."

"It's okay, Mom. You had no way of knowing." Jillian hadn't told her any of that to make her feel bad.

"Just don't give up." Her mother placed a jug of milk in the fridge.

"On what?" Surely she didn't mean Glenn.

"You know, on men in general. Just because you found one bad egg doesn't mean there isn't a prince out there waiting for you." Her mother was nothing if not resilient.

"I don't need a guy to complete me. I'm happy just the way I am."

"I know you don't need a man. Times are so much different these days. But that doesn't mean it wouldn't be nice to have someone to share your life with. Your father was my best friend. He knew me better than anyone. And I miss him every day."

Jillian wanted to ask her mother why she didn't take some of her own advice and get out there and start dating again, but she couldn't vocalize the words. If it was anyone but her mother, she would serve up some much needed advice. Her father had been gone for more than five years. It was time for her mother to move on.

But selfishly, Jillian found comfort in the fact her parents' love spanned not just life but death too. It was very special. And she also realized that she was a grown-up now and as hard as it might be, she needed to help her mother move on. Maybe tomorrow.

It was at this point that she noticed her mother walking around the kitchen looking high and low for something. "Did you lose something?"

"Did you see Romeo?"

"No. But I'm sure he's napping somewhere warm."

Her mother's face was creased with worry lines. "Romeo. Here, boy. Come to Momma."

Jillian stopped and listened for the now familiar sound of the pitter-patter of his tiny feet. But as the seconds ticked away, there was no rush of footsteps.

Perhaps he was curled up, snug in a blanket, and didn't feel like moving. As her mother continued to call for the cat, Jillian had a stroke of genius. She rushed over to the pantry and reached for a pouch of cat treats. This would work.

She jiggled the bag and waited.

Nothing.

Jillian moved to the living room and jiggled it again.

Still nothing.

Last try was in the hallway outside the bedrooms. *Jiggle. Jiggle.*

Not a murr or a purr.

And then Jillian had the worst flashback of when he'd snuck out the door at her place. As quickly as the thought came to her, she dismissed it. There was no way that cat would venture back out in the brutal cold. He would have learned his lesson. He was a very smart feline.

Besides, there was no way she was calling Avery, not after

the way he'd dismissed her during their last conversation. And she didn't want him thinking she'd made up this excuse in order to have a reason to call him. Romeo would be around here—somewhere.

"Hey, Mom, did you find him?" Jillian returned to the living room to find her mother down on her hands and knees checking under all of the furniture.

Her mother sat back on her heels. "No. And I'm worried."

"When did you last see him?"

"I don't know." She paused as though to give the question some thought. "I think it was when I left this morning." Her mother's eyes filled with unshed tears. "Do you think he got outside while I was carrying in the groceries?"

"No. He knows how cold it is out there."

"I hope you're right. I don't want to imagine him out in the dark, cold night." Her mother sniffled. "And he's not used to it. And...and it would be all my fault."

Now definitely wasn't the time for Jillian to confess about Romeo's prior excursion. It would just make her mother worry all the more and then she'd insist Jillian call Avery. And there was no way Romeo would be at Avery's house. He probably wouldn't even remember how to get there.

Jillian checked behind the couch for a second time. "Before you think the worst, we should keep checking here. He could have gotten closed in a cabinet or closet."

Her mother's eyes widened. "You're right. I'll start checking upstairs."

"And I'll search down here," Jillian said, already headed for the kitchen. "Yell, if you find him."

"You do the same," her mother called out.

In the kitchen, Jillian stopped next to the cabinet closest to the back door. Romeo was the curious sort and he had managed to pull open a cabinet door before. One by one, Jillian inspected the inside of each cabinet.

And then her phone buzzed. She thought of ignoring it, but then she realized that if Romeo had gotten out that her cell number was on his tag. She pulled the phone from the back pocket of her jeans. She glanced at the caller ID and found it was Avery.

Was it possible Romeo had actually made his way back to Avery's house?

Impossible.

She was about to let the call go to voicemail and deal with Avery later, but she couldn't ignore the fact that Avery might have seen Romeo roaming about town. Now, that was a very real possibility because Avery wouldn't have any other reason to call her.

On the fourth buzz, she pressed a button and lifted the phone to her ear. "Hello."

"Oh good. I was beginning to think you weren't going to answer."

"I'm a little busy." If this wasn't about Romeo, she really

didn't want to talk to him.

"You wouldn't by chance be looking for a little guy? You know, the black and white little dude that goes by the name of Romeo?"

"You've seen him?"

"In a manner of speaking. He came to my house and pawed at the door until I let him in."

"We've been looking everywhere for him. My mother is so upset. Is he okay?"

"He's perfectly fine."

"I'll be right over to get him."

"You don't have to rush. After a few pets, I fed him. And now he's in the living room with Marshmallow, warming up on a chair near the fireplace."

Jillian thanked Avery and then she went to find her mother. The time had come for that little confession about Romeo's previous excursion. Her mother wouldn't be too happy about her sweetie getting out and venturing across roads, but she would be immensely relieved that he was safe.

And then it would be up to Jillian to go pick him up. Whether she wanted to see Avery again or not, Romeo wasn't leaving her many options. Whatever made her think he would be a good lap cat?

Chapter Nine

H IS KNEE CONTINUED to ache.

Yet Avery refused to give in to the pain.

The physical therapist had assured him that each agonizing minute of his therapy was worth it. His strength and agility were improving. And soon he'd be fit and able to return to the rodeo. But now that he had the chance to own his own ranch, the rodeo circuit paled in comparison.

He'd had a lot of time to think while working in the kitchen. He wasn't as young as he used to be. And his body didn't bounce back from injuries as quickly as it once did. But he still had to come up with the money necessary to buy the ranch. He had some ideas, but nothing definite yet.

And he was making progress with the kitchen. In fact, at this rate, he'd be done in no time. He continued cutting brown, tan, gold, and cream metallic colored tiles to make a backsplash for the kitchen.

Fixing up the house had all started when a water pipe in the main bathroom began to leak and he had to knock out part of the wall. The project had rapidly expanded to updating the entire bathroom. The more he'd remodeled, the more he found that he liked working with his hands.

And now there was just the kitchen to complete and the house would be fully updated. In fact, it was good enough to fetch a generous price if he were to put it on the market. Guilt slugged him in the gut. How could he even consider selling the family home? But the devil on his shoulder whispered in his ear that Jordan had a whole new life in the Air Force and Beth had never actually said that she wanted to return to Marietta to live.

Avery shook his head. It didn't matter. He had no right to sell their parents' home for his own gain. He dismissed the thought even though the guilt lingered on.

He started the saw to cut the next section of tiles when he thought he heard something. He paused the saw and waited. But he didn't hear anything. He must have imagined it.

He restarted the saw and took his time cutting the tiles. He'd already learned the hard way how easy it was to mess them up and then have to go back to the hardware store to get more. And at this hour, the store was closed.

He focused his thoughts on the task at hand. One by one, the saw sliced through the colored glass, leaving behind a straight edge.

When he turned off the saw, there was knocking. This time he was certain he wasn't imagining it. And it was coming from the back door. It must be Jillian. Avery set aside his saw and moved toward the door.

"Hi." She sent him a hesitant smile. "I'm here to pick up Romeo."

"Come in." Avery stepped aside to let her pass.

"I'm really sorry he bothered you again."

Avery closed the door. "I think Romeo has a crush on Marshmallow."

"I don't know if I'd call it a crush." Jillian shifted the empty cat carrier from one hand to the other. "Can cats even have crushes?"

"Okay then, he's hot for her."

Jillian laughed. Her blue eyes lit up. They sparkled like sapphires. The breath hitched in his throat. There was something different about her this evening, but he couldn't put his finger on the change. Had she always been this beautiful?

"I don't think that's the right term." Jillian's words cut through his troubled thoughts. "I think he likes her. And I think she likes him too, but she isn't ready to admit it yet."

"I wonder if this is the beginning of a routine. At least you'll know where Romeo is when he escapes." Avery thought that would please Jillian, but she continued to frown. "What's wrong?"

"I just hate the thought of him crossing roads. It's so hard to see a black cat at night."

"He'll be fine."

"Says the man who almost ran him over."

Her words wounded Avery. Surely she knew how much he loved animals. "Hey, I wasn't even close."

Jillian's eyes widened. "How would you know? Remember, you never saw him?"

She did have a point, but he wanted to believe he hadn't been that close. The thought of hurting an innocent animal was quite upsetting.

"I see you're working on the kitchen." She glanced around. "It looks really nice. I like the green paint with the white trim. Are you replacing the appliances?"

He nodded. "I ordered them before my accident, when I thought my career was on the way up."

"It still can be. You just have to give your body time to heal. Speaking of which, I doubt you're supposed to be on your feet all day."

"I'm not one of the twins. You don't have to worry about me."

"If I don't, who will?" Jillian paused as though just now comprehending what she'd said. "Unless, of course, you're seeing someone."

He wasn't, but she was obviously involved with someone. "The only female in my life aside from Beth is Marshmallow. And she doesn't give me any grief unless I forget to feed her on time."

"Sounds about right." Jillian glanced around some more. "Are you almost finished?"

"I'm getting there."

"Are you installing recessed lighting beneath the cabinets?"

"Already installed." He walked over to the counter and flipped a switch. The new granite countertops were illuminated.

"Wow. Very nice."

As much as he hated to admit it, her compliment meant a lot to him. But it still rankled him that she was involved in a romantic relationship. He wished she'd mentioned it when he'd approached her about the tutoring. He would have backed off. Now everything was awkward.

"Thank you. I'm glad you like the changes," he said. "I thought it was time this place received a makeover."

"Any special reason?"

He shook his head. "I just wanted it nice for Beth."

"She's moving back here to Marietta after college?"

"I assumed she would." And then a thought struck him. "Is there something you know?"

Jillian shook her head. "She didn't say anything to me. I was just wondering with Beth always talking of the ocean if she would ever live in this house again."

Jillian's words triggered a lightbulb for him. He wasn't the only one striving to get away from here—from the memories of the family that had once been and was no more. He'd tried so hard to fill in for his parents, but he'd obviously failed as everyone wanted to go in a different direction.

As though Jillian could see the impact her words had on

him, she said, "Of course, I could totally be wrong about this."

He shook his head. "You're probably right. I guess I just didn't want to see how splintered our family has become. I bet that sounds really corny coming from me. After all, it's not like I'm their parent or anything."

"You've sacrificed a lot for them and they both love you so much."

It was more than he could process right now. He glanced quickly around the kitchen. It was coming together nicely, but it wasn't his style. He'd thought it was something Beth would enjoy. However, if Beth was never coming back, it was all for naught. But then again, it wouldn't be right to sell the only home they'd ever known. So what did he do now?

He shoved the quandary to the back of his mind. "We can talk in the living room."

Jillian shook her head. "I don't want to take up any more of your time when you're so busy. I can just grab Romeo and leave."

"I'm done for today." For some reason that he wasn't prepared to explore, he didn't want her to go. "And if you stay, it'll give me an excuse to sit down and put my leg up."

"Now how can I resist such a heartfelt offer?" She sent him a teasing grin.

He couldn't help but smile back at her. She had one of those smiles that was contagious. It was the first thing he'd noticed about her, way back in elementary school. She'd been a tomboy and adventurous. And now, she was definitely no longer a tomboy. He swallowed hard.

"How about some hot chocolate to warm you up." He had no idea where that offer came from. "And if you're lucky, there might still be some of those little marshmallows around here that Beth always has to have in her hot chocolate."

"Now, you've totally sold me. It's been a long time since I had little marshmallows."

"And here I thought it was the chocolate that women wanted."

"It is, but those marshmallows are the extra treats that make each cup perfect."

"Okay." He moved to the outlet to unplug the saw. "Glad you filled me in on the details or I never would have known."

"That's because you don't like marshmallows."

He could feel her gaze following him around the room as he gathered his tools. The truth was he wanted her to stay because he was lonely in this house. He wasn't used to it being so quiet.

"Would you like me to make the hot chocolate while you finish cleaning up?" she asked.

"Sure. If you don't mind."

In no time, his tools were picked up and the hot chocolate was made. They carried the cups into the living room where both cats sent them such innocent stares.

Marshmallow was seated on the cushion of the hunter green armchair, while Romeo looked quite comfortable on the arm of the chair. They were close, but not too close.

Avery glanced over at Jillian. A huge smile lit up her whole face. In that moment, he was certain she was the most beautiful woman he'd ever known. How had he missed it all of this time?

And then he realized he hadn't noticed because he hadn't been looking. He hadn't had a normal life. He hadn't dated like other men his age. Instead, he'd been busy raising a family. He'd been doing the science projects and mowing the grass when he wasn't working at the Crooked S or out on the rodeo circuit. His life had been one constant motion. And now he was standing perfectly still with no place for him to rush off to. And suddenly he was seeing all of the things he'd missed in the past.

And what he'd missed was how Jillian had grown into a beautiful woman. No wonder she had a boyfriend. It was surprising she wasn't married with a family of her own. But then again, she was focused on her career. Maybe they weren't as different as he'd thought.

"Aww...aren't they cute together?" Jillian said, jarring him from his thoughts. She rushed over and started to fuss over both cats.

Romeo murred as though in response to her question.

"It would appear he agrees with you." Avery smiled.

Jillian laughed as she moved back to Romeo. She

scratched under his chin. "You're a sweetie."

Avery just shook his head. "I think he has you wrapped around his tail."

"Oh no. Not me." She moved to the couch and sat down. "He's my mother's cat."

"And yet you're the one who ends up chasing him around Marietta."

Jillian took a sip of her hot chocolate and moaned in approval. "It's funny how that works, isn't it?"

"So how are things going with you?" He wondered if he was being too nosy. But it wasn't like he'd come straight out and asked her if it was serious with that guy she was kissing earlier today.

"They are good. In fact, they're real good."

He nodded. "Glad to hear it. I don't know if I mentioned it before but your shop is really nice. I'm sure it's already a huge hit with the residents, and when the rodeo is in town, you'll end up selling out."

"I don't know about that, but it sure would be nice. I've sunk everything I've got into it."

"It looks like your gamble is paying off," he said, regretful his life hadn't been different, but knowing he had no one to blame but himself.

"I'm still in a wait and see mode." She sipped her cocoa. "And how about you? Are you done with the rodeo?"

Done with the rodeo? That was a question to which he had no answer. If he could get his hands on the Crooked S, he'd give up the rodeo in a heartbeat. But securing the funding was still iffy.

"I don't know." It was as honest an answer as he could give her.

"Of course, you have to see how well your leg heals, especially since this isn't your first injury."

No, it wasn't. Far from it. Over the past ten years on the rodeo circuit, he'd sustained broken ribs, a busted collarbone, and a number of other injuries. His x-rays were a mess of scars. Still, he could only think of one other occupation he would like better—running his own ranch.

A murr from one of the cats had them both turning. Romeo finally made his way down onto the cushion of the chair next to Marshmallow. She immediately stood, gave him a slight hiss and left.

Avery couldn't help but chuckle at the dejected look on Romeo's face. "It's okay, buddy, women are hard to figure out."

"We are not." Jillian arched a brow at him.

"Yes, you are." Each time he ran into Jillian, he became increasingly confused about how she could so easily evoke emotions in him.

"What's so confusing? We want a career, a family, and a nice home. We want it all."

Avery's thoughts hovered on the fact she wanted a family. That's what he'd just dealt with for the past six years. It wasn't for the faint of heart. Being responsible for other people's well-being was a lot. Was it possible he'd misunderstood her?

He cleared his throat. "So you're looking forward to having a baby?"

"Someday." She paused as she stared at the fireplace. "I don't know if I'll ever have it all. But I refuse to settle for less."

Ouch. That left him out of any plans she might have for the future—not that he was thinking of being in her life. He inwardly groaned. How did they get on this subject anyhow?

"How about you?" she asked, drawing him out of his thoughts. "Are you planning on having a family of your own?"

"No." He didn't hesitate, not even for a split second. When her eyes widened in surprise, he added, "I already finished raising my brother and sister. That was enough for me."

"But it would be different if it was your own wife and child."

He shook his head. "I'm happy with the way things are now."

"You mean with you being out on the rodeo circuit?"

He shrugged. "Someday I'll retire."

"But not now?"

The thought of the Crooked S came to mind and so did the hefty price tag. "I don't know what the future holds."

She nodded in understanding and then proceeded to

switch the subject by asking, "How are your Bake-Off plans coming?"

"They aren't."

"You still have time. There's what—a couple of weeks until the big event starts?"

"I'm not going to do it."

A worried look came over her face. "Oh no. Everyone will be so disappointed, especially Harry's family."

"That's why I don't intend to tell them until I've found a suitable replacement."

"Oh." She stirred her hot chocolate. "You know I'm still available to help you."

"But you're so busy with your business. And I don't want to impose."

"You aren't imposing as I'm the one who's offering."

He hesitated. Should he go there? Sure, why not? It'd save them both some grief. "Won't your boyfriend get upset?"

"My boyfriend? I don't have one."

That surprised Avery. How would she define that man she was having a cozy moment with on the sidewalk? He was about to ask her, but he decided to refrain. While he composed himself and formulated an appropriate response, he preoccupied himself with taking a long drink of hot chocolate.

So if that guy he saw her with wasn't her boyfriend, then who was he? Because it sure looked to Avery that if this guy wasn't her boyfriend now, he certainly wanted to be in the very near future.

Still, she was single and offering him help. Not to mention Beth and the Monroes were counting on him. "You're sure you don't mind?"

"Avery, what's up with you? I've never had to repeat myself this much in the past. You know me. I don't offer unless I want to do something."

That much was true enough. She'd wanted to help when his parents died. At first, he thought she'd just taken the nanny position out of pity. But when he thought about her offer, he realized that she'd worked as a babysitter for his brother and sister since she was sixteen. If his parents had trusted her, why shouldn't he? In the end, it had been one of his best decisions.

He swallowed down the last of the hot chocolate. "You really think I should do this Bachelor Bake-Off?"

She nodded. "I do. Besides, it'll keep you from missing the rodeo, or at least help keep your mind off it for a little bit."

It was the problem of the ranch that was foremost in his mind. But that was a subject he didn't want to discuss. So far no one in town knew about the terms of the will and for now, he wanted it to stay that way.

He did not relish the idea of answering everyone's questions—especially when they'd want to know why he wasn't jumping on the offer to buy it. He didn't want to admit that he'd depleted his savings. He didn't want anyone pitying him.

"Then I accept the offer," he said, wondering if he was making a big mistake. "I'll pay you for your time."

"Pay me?" She shook her head. "I'm not doing it for the money."

"I have to repay you somehow." He watched as a myriad of expressions passed over her face. She had something on her mind and he wanted to know what it was because he didn't like being indebted to anyone. "What is it?"

"What are you talking about?"

"I saw that look on your face. You thought of some way for me to repay you. Tell me what it is and I'll do it."

She hesitated. "First, are you dating anyone?"

What in the world was she about to propose? His gut tightened, but he was already committed. "No, I'm not. Otherwise, I wouldn't have bothered you for baking lessons."

"Good point. Are you sure—"

"Jillian, out with it."

Her fine brows rose. "Be careful about agreeing to things without getting the details first." When he motioned for her to spit it out, she said, "I need an escort for a wedding."

This was not what he'd been expecting. He got to his feet and moved to the fireplace. A wedding? He didn't go to those things. In his limited experience, it always felt like if you weren't already part of a couple that people were trying to set you up.

And yet, he'd already told Jillian he'd do it. She did, after all, offer to help him even though she was busy starting up her own shop.

He turned to face her. He should tell her that he'd do it, but the words were stuck in the back of his throat. Of all the things she wanted, did it have to be this?

Jillian fidgeted with a silver ring on her middle finger. "I can tell by the look on your face that you'd rather have all of your teeth pulled out than do this." Disappointment reflected in her eyes. "Don't worry. You're off the hook."

"Is it really that important to you?"

She shrugged. "My mother RSVP'd that I'd be bringing someone."

"Can't you just tell them that you'll be alone?"

She shook her head. "The wedding is this weekend. With it being this close, everything has been planned out. But don't worry, it's not your problem."

It sure felt like his problem. He'd told her that he would do whatever she needed. "What happens if you go alone?"

"My mother has a fix for that. She wants to set me up with a friend's son. Did I mention that most of her friends are much older than my mother and therefore their sons are much older than me?"

"Ouch. Sorry about that." He supposed he could go for just a little bit. "But it won't be a date?"

"What won't be?"

He realized that he'd vocalized his thought. He cleared

his throat. "I'll go with you, but it won't be a date."

"But you don't have to—"

"We aren't going to have that conversation again, are we?"

Jillian smiled. "I suppose not. Thank you. And no, it's not a date. You'll just be my plus one."

Plus one? He thought about it for a moment. It didn't sound so bad. There were no romantic implications or anything.

His gaze met hers. "That's me. The plus one."

"Now that we have the details all worked out, how about we get started on the baking tomorrow evening? Because right now, I need to take Romeo home before my upset mother hunts us both down."

When she stood up to take her now empty mug to the kitchen, Avery stepped forward and held out his hand. "I can take it."

As she handed over the mug, their fingers touched. It sent the strongest sensation zinging up his arm. The fuzzy warm feeling settled in his chest before it emanated throughout his body. As their fingers continued to touch, his gaze met hers. Did she feel it too? She must have felt something or she wouldn't be looking at him the way she did.

And just like that snowy night not so long ago, he wondered what it would be like to kiss her. His gaze dipped to her lips. They were glossy and tempting.

Why exactly had he waited this long to kiss her? At that

particular moment, he couldn't remember. Whatever his reason, it didn't seem so important now.

His heart picked up its pace as he moved closer to her. All he could think about were her lips. It was time to put an end to all of the questions in his mind—

Thunk!

The sound of something falling drew Avery out of the spell Jillian had cast over him. All too soon, she withdrew her hand from his. Disappointment assailed him.

They both turned to find a stack of magazines from the coffee table had fallen to the floor. Romeo sat on the coffee table and stared down at the mess.

Avery cleared his now dry throat. "I'll clean it up as soon as I take these to the kitchen."

He moved to the kitchen and placed the mugs in the sink. He couldn't help but wonder what would have happened if the cat hadn't interrupted them. Would Jillian have welcomed his kiss? It really bothered him that he'd never know.

Avery drew in a deep, calming breath and then returned to the living room. He was immediately greeted by unhappy meows. "What's going on in here?"

Jillian held out the cat carrier. "Just to be sure that Romeo doesn't pull another disappearing act tonight, my mother sent along his cat carrier. As you can tell, he's not too fond of it."

"Marshmallow doesn't like those things either. She howls

the whole way to the vet's office."

"How's Marshmallow doing now that no one is home much?"

He shrugged. "She's not too crazy about it. She stays at my neighbor's house. Luckily, the older woman next door loves cats and doesn't mind taking in one more from time to time. I don't think Marshmallow likes the other cats over there, but I don't have any other options at this point."

Jillian started for the front door. "If you ever need someone else to take Marshmallow, perhaps my mother could try it. Obviously Romeo wouldn't mind. I'm just not so sure Marshmallow is as fond of him."

They both smiled.

"I'll keep that in mind. It might be best." When Jillian briefly frowned, he couldn't help asking, "Why don't you look happy about that? If you think it'd be too much for her—"

"It's not that." Jillian shook her head. "Never mind."

"Talk to me, Jillian."

"I was just thinking that if you didn't have Marshmallow you'd be all alone."

Oh. Is that all? He breathed a little easier. "It's not bad being alone. You should know."

"I'm not alone. Trust me. Now that I live next door to my mother, I see her every single day and she has me babysitting Romeo any chance she can. She's worried that he'll get lonely." Jillian rolled her eyes. "This isn't good."

"What isn't?"

"I just realized I'm turning into my mother."

He chuckled. "That isn't such a bad thing. I like your mother."

"Thanks. But no one wants to turn into their parent. And yet, I'm bothering you about ending up old and alone like she does with me. Ugh!" Jillian pulled open the door. "On that note, I'll say goodnight."

Avery watched her go and realized he was still smiling. For the first time since he'd returned home, he'd actually enjoyed himself. But he knew not to get used to having Jillian around. They wanted very different things in life.

While she longed to be tied down with a baby, he'd already raised a family. He may be anticipating the commitment of a ranch, but that was far different than the pressures of a family—of always wondering if he was doing a good enough job as a guardian or a parent.

The truth was he didn't feel worthy of his own family. He'd already done so much damage to the family he had with his parents and siblings. If only he'd done things differently—

Chapter Ten

J ILLIAN YAWNED.

For the most part, sleep had evaded her the night before as she'd contemplated the pros and cons of the deal she'd just made with Avery. His presence at the wedding would hopefully make her mother happy. As for her relatives, they'd probably still comment about her being the last single female of her cousins. Didn't they know that train of thought was antiquated?

But the part that concerned her the most was that if not for Romeo, she and Avery would have kissed the night before. Just the memory of the way Avery had stared at her made her insides shiver with excitement. How was it possible that he'd slipped past her very carefully laid defenses?

She swallowed hard as she considered this serious turn of events. And the way she saw it was that their chance of happiness had passed them by. Whatever happened last night had been a fluke—a glimpse of what might have been. It didn't change things.

She was over Avery. He was a friend. Nothing more.

Exceptionally tired that morning, not even the two mugs of coffee had pumped her up. She yawned countless times as she drove to work. The shop door jingled as she let herself inside. Suzanna was already hard at work painting a figurine.

"Good morning," Suzanna said cheerily followed by a bright, glowing smile.

"Don't you ever sleep in?" Jillian grumbled.

"Not when I have things I want to do." Suzanna studied her. "I take it you didn't have a good night."

Jillian shrugged. "Too much on my mind."

"Anything I can help with?"

This was as good as any time to tell her friend the latest development. "I've agreed to give Avery baking lessons."

"Oh." Suzanna turned back to her project.

"Is that all you're going to say?"

"What do you want me to say?"

"I don't know." Jillian sighed. "I keep wondering if this is a big mistake."

"Because you're not as immune to Avery's charms as you want to believe?"

"I'm over him," she said too quickly.

"Uh-huh." Suzanna's tone was one of disbelief.

"Why do you have to say it like that?"

"Like what?" Suzanna said all innocently.

"Like there's more going on than baking lessons?"

"Well, isn't there?"

"No. It's not like that."

Suzanna nodded her head, but her eyes said that she wasn't buying anything Jillian said.

"I'm so over him," Jillian insisted. It was time to turn the tables. "And what about you? Isn't it time you had another date?"

Suzanna shook her head. "I've tried and I'm done."

Jillian knew how hard it was for Suzanna to put herself out there. She'd been hurt badly when she'd been jilted at the altar. But Jillian also knew that deep inside Suzanna was a romantic. And Jillian didn't want Suzanna's creep of an ex to steal her friend's chance at happily ever after.

"Not everyone is like—"

"This isn't about me," Suzanna said, taking time to rearrange a few items in the jewelry display case. "You're just trying to avoid the subject of your date with Avery."

They weren't going on a date. Not even close. The bake lessons were for a good cause. It had nothing to do with how cute Avery looked or how he was starting to acknowledge his appreciation of her.

Suzanna set aside her paintbrush. "So when are these lessons to start?"

"Tonight. We don't have much time. The competition is in less than two weeks."

"Really? Why is there such a rush?"

"From what I've learned from my mother, there's a problem with the sale of the house they plan to use for the kids' center. And the committee has less than ninety days in which to come up with money for the repairs or else the Chamber of Commerce is going to let an outside business take over the place."

"I don't like the sounds of an outsider coming in."

"Me either. That's why just about everyone in town is planning to support the Bake-Off in one manner or another. Speaking of which, those wristbands I ordered should arrive soon."

"Actually, there was a delivery for you this morning."

"Good. Where are they?"

"I don't think it's the wristbands."

"I didn't order anything else that I can think of, but then again I've had a lot on my mind."

"I put the box in the office on the desk."

Jillian moved to the office. She hung up her coat and turned to the desk to find a white oblong box with a big red bow. That box definitely didn't contain wristbands. Her guess was that it contained flowers. From Avery?

Her heart picked up its pace. Was it possible she'd totally misjudged him? Did agreeing to teach him to bake create that big of a response in him?

She rushed over to the desk and slid the bow from the box. Inside were a dozen long-stem red roses. They were absolutely gorgeous. She'd only received roses from one other guy and that had been Glenn after their first date. He'd done everything he could to turn her head and it had worked, until she refused to let him control her life.

There was a little white envelope enclosed. She withdrew it and slid out the note.

I know that we're meant to be.

Give me another chance.

Glenn

Jillian's heart sunk. She slid the card back in the envelope. Did he really think that after the way he'd publicly dumped her that this would make up for things?

When she returned to the showroom, Suzanna glanced her way. "So which man are they from?"

"Glenn. Can you believe that? He breaks up with me one minute and the next he wants me back."

"That's because he came to his senses and realized what an amazing woman he gave up." When Jillian didn't respond, Suzanna asked, "Do you think there's more to this?"

Jillian shook her head. "I think I didn't get enough sleep last night and my imagination is running wild. Enough of that. It's time to get to work. The first thing I'm going to do is find out where those wristbands are."

DON'T MAKE A *big deal of this.*

That evening, Jillian stopped running the vacuum over the floor—for the second time. After all, it was only Avery coming over. It wasn't like they hadn't known each other forever.

But this was different. She was no longer his employee and there were no longer energetic kids pulling them in opposite directions. And that made this feel more—ugh, what was the word she was searching for? Intimate? No. Special? Maybe. But there was another description just beyond her reach for how she felt about this evening.

Jillian returned the vacuum to the closet. She glanced around the living room. Everything was in its proper place, thanks to Romeo not being there. She'd quickly learned that he enjoyed rearranging her decorations, especially anything round or lightweight. But this evening, her mother's favorite show was on television so Romeo would be busy helping her mother knit. Jillian smiled at the thought. Her mother spent more time untangling Romeo from the yarn than she did knitting, but they both seemed to enjoy it.

Jillian glanced down at her outfit, wondering if it would do. She'd switched her clothes three times now. When she'd arrived home after closing up Tangled Charms at a few minutes after six, she'd immediately changed into her usual jeans and a sweatshirt. However, that just didn't feel right. So then she'd put on some fresh work clothes consisting of black slacks and a white blouse, but that felt too dressy—like she was trying too hard to impress him.

After another search of her closet, she'd settled on a fuzzy purple sweater and dark jeans. It wasn't dressy but it wasn't too casual. It was something that she'd wear to a friend's house or FlintWorks for a night out.

Before she could change her mind again, there was a knock at the door. Avery was early. She'd forgotten that about him.

She rushed to the door; all the while her stomach shivered with nerves. *Stop freaking out! Everything will be fine.* Jillian paused and took a deep breath.

She swung the door wide open. "Hi, Avery. Come on in. Don't mind the mess."

He glanced around. "What mess?"

Erm, she was nervous and had uttered the first thing that came to mind. "Oh, um, I guess I got it all picked up."

"This is the first time I've been in your new place." He glanced at the galley kitchen and then the living room. "It's smaller than your house, but it has a lot of character."

"Thanks. My mother was between tenants at just the right time. We, or rather I, remodeled the place and made it my own. One of the perks of being related to the owner."

"If I'd have known you were this good, I would have asked you for some remodeling tips for the house."

This casual conversation was helping her to relax. "You definitely didn't need my help. You did a fantastic job. What did Beth and Jordan have to say about all of your hard work?"

"Well, Jordan hasn't seen any of it because he didn't get leave at Christmas." Avery glanced down. "Beth picked out paint colors."

"I'm sure she loved the rest of your work. The house has a whole new, more modern feel."

He shrugged. "You know how kids are, always on their phone or running off to meet friends."

So Beth hadn't noticed how much time and attention to detail her brother had put into the house. Jillian felt bad for him. "Well, I think what you did is amazing. I'm sure when their lives slow down a bit, they'll appreciate all of your hard work."

He grunted as though he didn't agree. "Should we get started?"

She glanced around and realized he hadn't brought any supplies. "Can I help you carry anything in?"

He sent her a blank look. "Carry what?"

"Oops. I guess there was a miscommunication. I thought you had what you wanted to bake and just needed some help learning how to put it all together."

He shook his head. "I need help with all of it. I have no idea what to bake."

"I see." Well, that certainly cast a different glow over the evening. "I'm afraid my baking supplies are a little low—"

"No problem. I planned to go shopping as soon as I figure out what I need." He raked his fingers through his hair, sending the longer waves scattering. "I guess I didn't make that clear when we spoke."

"Do you know what types of baked goods you have to make?"

He yanked a folded paper from his jeans pocket. "This is everything I know about the event."

Jillian accepted the paper and unfolded it. She scanned down over the Bake-Off guidelines. There were to be three events. All baking was to be done at the competition. No at-home-baked items permitted. Each participant was to bake cookies, a pie, and a cake.

"The cookies don't sound so bad," she said, still reading the comments on the paper. "You just have to pick a recipe. The cake will be a bit harder." She paused as her gaze scanned back to the list of baked items. There weren't many details. "Do you know if the pie crust has to be from scratch?"

He frowned. "Everything has to be done from scratch."

"Uh-huh."

Avery's frown deepened. "What does uh-huh mean?"

"It just means that some of this will be harder than other items."

"Translated to mean that I'm in big trouble here."

"Don't freak out. I'll help you get through it." She re-folded the paper and handed it back to him. "I have some cookbooks over here." She walked toward the kitchen area. It was a good thing she'd borrowed some of her mother's cookbooks. Most of hers were in storage as this efficiency apartment didn't allow for a lot of extras. "We can go through them and see if anything strikes your fancy."

They sat down on the matching barstools and started

flipping through page after page of recipes. It soon became obvious that it would be best to tackle each round of the competition separately. It might help Avery not feel so totally overwhelmed—kind of how he looked right now. She felt bad for him.

Jillian glanced down at her notepad. "So you've narrowed the cookie recipes down to chocolate chip, snickerdoodles, or cowboy cookies. Which one shall we try first?"

Avery flipped through the cookbooks to the pages with the sticky tabs. He hemmed and hawed a bit as he turned the pages back and forth. She couldn't help but smile. She'd never known anyone to put such effort into picking out a recipe.

And then he sat back and looked at her. "I think I like the sound of cowboy cookies best of all. It's rather fitting, don't you think?"

"I do. But what about the other recipes? Do you want to try them?"

"Only if the cowboy cookies don't work out."

"Okay, then we have a plan." She got to her feet. "Next stop the grocery store."

He sent her a lazy smile that made her stomach flutter. "At least this part I know how to do." He moved to the door and pulled his keys from his pocket. "Let's go."

"Um, aren't you going to write down the ingredients first?"

He sighed and shook his head. "See what happens when I go and open my mouth?"

He sat back down and started writing out the ingredients.

This was going to be a very interesting evening. And a longer one than she'd anticipated, but fortunately she didn't have anything else planned—except for working on her special contribution to the fundraiser.

THIS FEELS SO natural.

But how is that possible?

Avery had never gone grocery shopping with Jillian. He'd always gone alone while she was watching the kids. And now, here he was pushing a shopping cart down the aisle of the Monroe Grocery Store while Jillian made small talk about the Bake-Off.

He nodded or gave a one-word response at the appropriate spots. He hadn't told Jillian, but he hated grocery shopping. These days he did it rarely and grudgingly. Most of the time he opted for takeout from one of the local restaurants.

No sir. He didn't like grocery shopping at all. It made him think of when he was struggling to finish raising his brother and sister. And in the solitude of grocery shopping, he had too much time to think.

And today his thoughts had drifted to his visit to the bank first thing that morning. He knew securing a loan to buy the Crooked S wouldn't be easy, but he didn't expect a quick and firm denial. Being a rodeo cowboy, he was classified as self-employed. To make a living, he had to be out on the road and thus unavailable to run the ranch. And the bank didn't believe he'd be able to turn the ranch's finances around quick enough, especially if he were to split his time between the ranch and the rodeo. They deemed the venture too high risk. Still, Avery refused to give up.

Lost in his thoughts, he didn't realize Jillian had stopped in front of him. The cart he was pushing ran right into her. She let out a small ompf before turning in his direction and leveling him with a frown.

"Sorry," he said hesitantly.

And then she surprised him by smiling. "Is grocery shopping that boring to you?"

"It's not exactly enjoyable."

"Really? I love it. Except when I'm hungry. Those are the times I buy far more than I intended and my credit card cringes. Not to mention half of my loot isn't exactly on the healthy side of life."

It was hard to remain in a foul mood when he was with Jillian. "Ah…so you're a junk food junkie."

She shrugged. "I call it fun food."

He laughed, liking this less serious side of Jillian. "And does changing the name make it healthier?"

"So anyway, what's first on our shopping list?"

He shook his head. "Oh no, you aren't going to change the subject. I'm curious about this."

"There's nothing to be curious about."

"Oh yes, there is. You've always been so perfect in school, at home, and with your business. So I really enjoy hearing about this rebel side of you. So what's your favorite? Chips? Ice cream? Candy?"

A rosy hue came over her cheeks. "Avery, do you have to? It's not that big of a deal."

"It must be or you wouldn't be blushing." His smile broadened. "You know, I'm beginning to see how much fun this grocery shopping can be."

He'd definitely been doing it wrong all of this time. He should have been shopping with Jillian. Perhaps he'd see about them shopping together in the future. The idea definitely had possibilities.

"Avery," came a voice from behind him.

He turned to see Mrs. Monroe approaching him. Her arms were outstretched and before he knew it, he was enveloped in a warm hug. It'd been a long time since anyone had hugged him. He remembered vividly at his parents' funeral how everyone in town had shown up. With most of them knowing him since he was in diapers, a handshake just wouldn't do. There was hug after hug. At the time, he'd been so numb that he was able to get through it.

After the funeral, he hadn't been able to take the coddling any longer. He had been angry at the world for stealing away two healthy people who had a loving family counting on them. Avery had distanced himself from people except for his brother and sister, but they had never been a touchy-feely family.

Marietta was such a small town. Everyone knew everyone else, and they all wanted to comfort him, but in reality, no one could. The devastating loss of his parents was something he and his siblings had to get through on their own—in their own time.

The love and caring of the town had been smothering. He knew how that sounded—awful. But it's how he'd felt for the longest time. And with a brother and sister to finish raising, he had to concentrate on their needs. They were the reason he kept putting one foot in front of the other.

He was surprised to find that Mrs. Monroe's hug didn't bother him. Maybe it was because she'd just gone through a similar horrific experience with the loss of her son. Or maybe he'd finally healed and was ready to move on with the rest of his life.

Mrs. Monroe pulled back and there were tears in her eyes. "When I heard what you volunteered to do, I was so touched." She swiped the moisture from her eyes. "Harry would have really liked it too. I just know that he'll be smiling down over the Bake-Off."

"I...I'm happy to do what I can. But I have to admit it wasn't my idea."

"It's okay. I know my daughter and your sister lassoed you into this, but you didn't have to agree. So I'm thankful."

Avery shifted uncomfortably. He didn't feel as though he deserved such high praise, especially after he'd nearly backed out of the whole event. "I hope you don't expect much. I've never mastered baking."

"Just you being there and making the effort will be enough for me and everyone else." And then Mrs. Monroe noticed Jillian. "Hello, Jillian. I'm so sorry I haven't had a chance to visit Tangled Charms, but I will soon. I've heard amazing reviews about the place. And I've seen people wearing your jewelry. It's so beautiful."

Jillian's cheeks glowed pink again. "Thank you. I understand you have a lot on your hands right now. Don't worry. I plan on the store being there for many years. You can stop by any time that's convenient for you."

Mrs. Monroe got a puzzled look on her face. "Do you need help finding something?"

Jillian shook her head. "Thanks. But I think I've got everything under control."

Avery watched as Jillian began moving away from him as she perused the shelf of canned soup. What in the world? He wondered why she didn't admit that she was there with him. Was she worried he wouldn't want Mrs. Monroe to know she was helping him with the Bake-Off?

He didn't mind at all. The more honest he was with Harry's mother, the better he felt about Harry's family putting up the money to sponsor him in this Bake-Off. Truthfully, he wished they would sponsor someone else— someone who knew his way around a cake pan—but obviously that wasn't going to happen.

He cleared his throat, regaining Mrs. Monroe's attention. "Actually, Jillian is here with me. She's going to help, erm, mentor me for the Bake-Off."

"She is?" Mrs. Monroe's gaze moved between the two of them.

He nodded. "She agreed to be with me every step of the way."

"That's so nice of her. You make sure you treat her well."

Treat her well? What was that supposed to mean? Was he supposed to insist on paying her? Was going to the wedding enough?

"I'll definitely do my best," he said, hoping that was the right thing to say. He noticed that Jillian was studying the store list as though she had to cram for a surprise exam.

"I'm sure you will." Mrs. Monroe smiled.

Was it his imagination or had there been a distinctive gleam in the woman's eyes? He turned to Jillian whose cheeks were rosy red. He was obviously missing something, but for the life of him, he couldn't figure out what it was.

AND SO IT begins.

Jillian's good mood evaporated. Thankfully Mrs. Monroe had been called away, but it was too late. The gossip was going to start up again. She fully expected the whispers, hopeful looks, and innuendos about her and Avery being a couple.

And Avery had done nothing to discourage Mrs. Monroe from thinking they were romantically involved. Didn't he see what he was doing? Surely he wasn't that oblivious, was he?

Back when Jillian had worked for him, things had gotten cozy. As one year rolled into the next, they had gotten closer. At least she thought they had.

There had been movie nights that he'd invited her to—but then again, as she thought back over it, perhaps it had been Beth who had invited her and Avery had merely agreed. There had been informal dinners and school events.

Was it possible she'd read too much into the past? Probably. She'd made a fool of herself for Avery and he acted as though he never even noticed. But she was a little older now and hopefully a lot wiser.

Okay, so she had dated Glenn and that hadn't exactly been one of her smarter moves. Still, it did prove that she was over her crush on Avery.

She was a business owner now. She needed the town to take her seriously, not gossip about how she kept making a mess of her love life.

Jillian took off down the grocery store aisle. She could hear Avery call her name, but she didn't want to stop—not yet. She had to calm herself so she didn't say something that she'd later regret.

When she stepped into the aisle with the baking supplies, she glanced at the list. She needed chocolate chips. She grabbed the name-brand milk chocolate ones. In her opinion, there was no skimping when it came to chocolate.

When she turned to place the chocolate chips in the cart, her gaze strayed across Avery. His expression was stormy and lines of frustration were written all over his face.

"Are you going to talk to me?" he asked.

"Yes." Just not about what was bothering her. "Do you see the flaked coconut around here?"

He moved around the cart toward her. "I don't want to talk about the shopping list."

"But we need to find this stuff—"

He placed his hand on hers. "What we need is for you to tell me what happened back there."

Her gaze moved from his face to his hand. As though he realized he was now holding her hand, he withdrew his hand. She couldn't believe he didn't know what was going on.

"I'm not having this conversation here," she said firmly.

"But why? I don't understand. I was just giving you credit for helping me get through this competition. I thought mentioning your contribution would have made you happy."

"It's not that."

"Then what is it?"

"It's—nothing. Forget it." She moved away from him to

continue their shopping. Thankfully their list was short so it shouldn't take them too long.

Avery cleared his throat. "Is there anything I can help with?"

"Yes, we need parchment paper. I'm out."

"Parchment paper? I'm guessing that's not with the construction paper."

She couldn't help but smile. "No. Try the aisle with the aluminum foil and plastic wrap."

"I'll be back."

While he was off on that task, she consulted the store list again. She kept losing her train of thought. She moved down the baking aisle, searching for the coconut. At last, she spotted it. She grabbed a bag of the generic stuff. In this case, generic would do.

She turned around and nearly bumped into Avery. She jumped back. "I didn't hear you."

"Must be my stealth abilities." He grinned at her.

"Uh-huh. Well, you can have this." She handed over the coconut.

Avery's face scrunched up in obvious disgust. "What's this for?"

Was he serious? "It's for your cookie recipe. Is that a problem?"

He was still frowning. "Uh, I guess not."

She pressed her hands to her hips. "We seem to be experiencing another lack of communication. What's up with the frowny face?"

He shrugged. "I don't like coconut."

"But you picked out the recipe. Didn't you read over the ingredients?"

"Not really."

"So what did you do? Go by the photo?"

He nodded. "The pretzels and chocolate chips looked good."

Well, she supposed that was something. Perhaps they could modify the recipe a bit. "Let me have that coconut back."

He handed it over and watched as she returned it to the shelf. "But I thought we needed it."

"Not if you don't like it—"

"But the recipe—"

"Can be modified." She glanced down at the store list in her hand. She might as well find out if they were going to have any other problems. "How do you feel about oats?"

He shrugged.

Not a good sign. She scratched them.

"How about pecans?"

He shook his head. "I don't like nuts in my food."

She was tempted to ask why he'd chosen this particular recipe since he obviously didn't like most of the ingredients, but she knew the answer—he was drawn in by the name, cowboy cookies. Sometimes men could be such little boys.

There had to be a way to fix this. There was nothing in

the Bake-Off rules she was given that said they couldn't make up their own recipe. And it didn't make sense to have Avery bake something he wouldn't eat.

With her mind made up, she said, "Okay. Pick out a couple ingredients you would enjoy in your cookie."

"What do you mean?"

"Not the eggs and flour and stuff, but rather what you'd like to replace the coconut and pecans with."

"Oh. Okay." He started down the aisle. He stopped at the end and held up a bag of Reese's Pieces. "I like these."

She had to admit that this totally confused her. "But you just got done telling me you don't like nuts in your food."

"But these aren't nuts. They're different."

"It's peanut butter."

"But it's a different texture and doesn't taste the same."

Was he serious? By the look on his face, he was. She reached for the bag and placed it in the cart. "What else?"

He looked around and she pointed out a few things. He ended up keeping the pretzels and chocolate chips that were mentioned in the recipe. Okay, it wasn't the total disaster she was anticipating. These ingredients were things she could work with.

By the time they finished their tour through the store, they had everything they needed for the cookies, and in the process Jillian had picked up her weekly store order. She noticed that Avery hadn't picked up any extras to take home with him. She considered asking him about it, but she decided to just let it go.

This was a new area for them and she wasn't sure what the boundaries were in this newfound relationship. Was she just to be his mentor? Or were they going to try to resurrect their prior friendship? It was all a bit confusing.

Chapter Eleven

THIS WAS A mistake.

Avery insisted on carrying the groceries into Jillian's apartment. It was the least he could do. This whole evening wasn't going as smoothly as he'd hoped. Something had shifted between them since running into Mrs. Monroe, and Jillian refused to talk about it. Even joking around with her to add some levity to the situation hadn't fixed things—at least not permanently.

Had Jillian changed her mind about working with him? The thought didn't sit well with him and it had nothing to do with winning the Bake-Off.

Avery placed the groceries on the counter, not quite sure what to say next. Perhaps it was best to give Jillian some space. "Thanks for shopping with me. You know, if you have other things to do, I could take all of this and get out of your way."

Her eyes widened as though she was surprised that he was trying to back out. "You've already changed your mind about the Bake-Off?"

"No. I'm going to do it. I just—well, you didn't seem happy about it when I mentioned us working together on it to Mrs. Monroe."

"I told you not to worry about it." Jillian busied herself by putting away the groceries.

"What was it? Why did my speaking with Mrs. Monroe bother you?"

"It wasn't you talking to her that bothered me. I…I just didn't want her to think I was doing something wrong by helping you with the Bake-Off."

He breathed his first easy breath. "That's what you were worried about?"

She nodded.

"Then don't worry. When I was out and about earlier today, I ran into Carol Bingley. She told me all of the bachelors had solicited help in one manner or another." If that was all that bothered her about this arrangement, then maybe they could keep going.

"Oh." She didn't seem that surprised or relieved. "That's good to hear."

"But if you're still uncomfortable, you can back out. I'd understand."

She shook her head. "Stay. We have some cookies to bake."

And so Avery found the recipe in the cookbook and Jillian gathered the ingredients. Her kitchen was a lot smaller than his and thus a lot cozier. They nearly collided a few times.

"A lot of recipes call for two bowls. I usually don't do it that way, especially for cookies." Jillian took a seat on the other side of the bar from him. "I usually start with the butter. And since you've switched up the recipe, I wondered if you'd like to try something else."

Since he didn't have a clue what he was doing, what was one more change to the recipe? "Sure. What did you have in mind?"

"I thought we could brown the butter?"

His nose instinctively retracted. "Why would we do that?"

She smiled at him. "It will caramelize it. You do like caramel, don't you?"

He nodded. "Just show me what to do."

She walked him through the process. It certainly seemed easy enough. He made notes on a slip of paper so he could repeat the process. Once the butter turned an amber shade, Jillian explained how to cool it in a cold-water bath.

Jillian continued to instruct him on what to do and when. So far so good. After the eggs and vanilla were mixed, it was time for the flour. Avery dumped a full cup in with the mixer on medium speed. Instantly, there was a white cloud of flour.

"Stop the mixer!" Jillian waved her hands and jumped off the stool.

"Oops! I guess I wasn't supposed to do that," he said,

inspecting the mess he'd made.

Jillian glanced down at her flour-covered clothes and then her gaze moved to him. He looked down to find that he was wearing a layer of flour too. He wasn't sure how angry Jillian was with him. The flour was not only on them but also the counter, the cookbooks, and the floor. It was everywhere.

The longer she remained quiet, the more worried he became. He was in so far over his head with this whole baking thing. And this proved it.

"I'm so sorry," he said. "I'll clean it up."

Suddenly she burst out laughing. It wasn't a small, polite giggle. This was a full-on belly laugh. Her eyes grew shiny with happy tears. And it was contagious. He couldn't help but laugh too. He had no idea why they were laughing, but it did feel good.

Jillian had a warm laugh that put him at ease. He couldn't help but think she needed to laugh more. Her face was full of color and her eyes sparkled with merriment.

It was in that moment he realized how much he missed hearing her laughter around his house. Since she'd quit working for him, the house seemed so much quieter and a lot emptier. This Bake-Off was turning into an eye-opening experience. Maybe this freedom thing wasn't all it was cracked up to be.

Jillian brushed off her sweater and then turned to him. "Here, let me help you."

She started to brush off his chest. Her hands running over his body made him think of what it would be like to pull her close and taste her berry lips. His gaze dipped to her mouth and her plump lower lip. She definitely had a mouth that was begging to be kissed.

He should glance away, but he couldn't because in that moment all he could think about was her tempting lips. He'd be willing to guess they would be sweeter than the cookies he was about to bake.

Her hands stilled over his heart as she worked at removing a bit of splattered dough. She was causing his heart rate to skyrocket. He wondered if she could feel it. And if she could, what was she thinking? What would she do if he were to swoop in and press his mouth to hers?

He raised his hand until it covered hers. His thumb stroked the back of her hand. He noticed the softness of her skin. The breath hitched in the back of his throat.

When his gaze met hers, he found questions swirling within the depths of her big blue eyes. He probably had some of the same questions. Where was this going? And what did he expect?

But he had absolutely no answers—not for her—and not for himself. Until he did have some answers, perhaps he should proceed with caution for both of their sakes. Because the very last thing he wanted to do was hurt Jillian.

He grudgingly pulled his hand away, hoping the lack of contact would return his heart rate to a normal pace. And that his thoughts would focus on anything but kissing her.

She moved away without saying a word. Maybe she hadn't noticed his slipup. Could he be that lucky?

"Did you add the salt?" she asked.

He thought about it for a moment. "No."

"It's in the cabinet next to the stove." Just then her phone chimed. "It's a text. I better check it."

Avery welcomed the distraction. He moved to the cabinet and quickly found a container marked salt. After consulting the recipe, he measured out a teaspoon and mixed it in with the rest of the ingredients.

Jillian set aside her phone. "It was nothing important." She picked up the salt. "Is this what you used?"

Oh no. That didn't sound good. "Um...yeah."

She frowned.

"I take it that isn't the right thing."

She shook her head. "This is coarse salt. I use it for things like the top of pretzels."

"I'll just toss this out." He picked up the bowl and started for the trash.

"No. Don't."

Avery paused. "I don't understand. You just said I used the wrong stuff."

"But the beautiful thing about baking and cooking is the ability to be flexible and make recipes your own."

"So the coarse salt is fine?"

"I don't know, but we're going to find out." Jillian retrieved the measuring cup for the flour. "Perhaps you should hand stir it for a bit."

He sighed. "This is what I was worried about. I'm a disaster in the kitchen."

Jillian smiled. "No, you're not. I think a lot of people put in too much flour all at once and learn the same lesson you did. In the future, you'll be sure to remember to add the flour in smaller portions."

"I hope so. Talk about a mess."

"I did it when I was a kid and I didn't forget."

He glanced around. "I feel really bad that your kitchen is a mess."

She waved off his worry. "It's nothing that can't be cleaned up."

And so back to work he went. By the time he carefully dropped each spoonful of cookie dough onto the cookie sheet and slipped it in the oven, he was feeling more confident about his baking skills. Jillian had more patience than he was expecting. The fact she hadn't freaked out over the mess he'd made shocked him. She was going to make someone an awesome mom.

He could envision her with a baby in her arms. A little girl who looked just like her. And then he pictured himself as part of that image—the loving husband and doting father—

Wait. What?

Totally confused by the direction of his thoughts, he gave himself a mental shake. What was up with him? Maybe it was this intimate setting. Yes, that had to be it. Jillian's place was a lot different than his parents' house. This apartment was warm and snug like a love nest. While his parents' home was more formal.

Once the dishes were washed up and the remnants of flour removed from the kitchen, Jillian invited him to sit with her in the living room area of the open floor plan. The last batch of cookies was in the oven. He really just wanted to leave.

Still, he couldn't be rude and run out on her, especially after the way she'd gone out of her way to help him. And so he took a seat on the couch, leaving a respectable space between them. He sat there for a moment in silence, not sure what to say.

"What's bothering you?" Jillian's voice cut through his thoughts.

"Why do you think anything's wrong?"

"Because I've known you most of my life and I can tell when something's eating at you."

He wasn't about to tell her the truth—that she made him wonder what his life would be like if his parents hadn't died. If he'd had a normal life, would they have ended up together? Would they have had a baby together?

Instead he uttered, "I got a letter this week."

"That must have been some letter to rattle you so much."

Now why in the world had he gone and mentioned the letter? He'd planned to keep it to himself until he'd made a decision. But he found it surprisingly easy to talk to Jillian—as long as it didn't involve his mixed emotions about her.

"It was definitely a shock." He raked his fingers through his hair. "It appears Howard Smith set up his will in such a way that I was given first chance at buying the Crooked S Ranch."

"Really?" Her face lit up with a big smile. "That's wonderful. Mr. Smith always did treat you like family. So what does this mean?"

"That's the problem. His nephews are businessmen in San Francisco and they have no interest in running a ranch. They want to sell it and I have ninety days in which to secure financing."

"I'm so happy for you." She studied his face. When he didn't respond, she asked, "Why don't you seem excited about this?"

"Believe me, I am. I'm just worried."

Her smile dimmed as concern reflected in her eyes. "Worried about what?"

"Coming up with the money. I already talked to the bank and I've been turned down for a loan."

"Well, if that's the problem, there has to be another solution." She leaned back on the couch as though to consider the options.

"Don't worry about it. This is my problem."

"But sometimes two minds are better than one."

Just then the timer for the cookies went off. Avery

jumped to his feet. When he pulled the cookies from the oven, he said, "I think I've got these cookies down pat."

"Good." Jillian joined him in the kitchen. She grabbed one of the cookies and took a bite. "Mm... Did you taste them?"

"I had some of the batter."

"You need to try the baked version." She grabbed another cookie and held it out to him.

He took it and bit into the still-warm cookie. It was a mix of different textures. The soft chocolate, the crunchy pretzel, and the rich, chewy cookie dough. He liked it. Really liked it.

He couldn't help but smile. He'd actually accomplished this—with a little bit of help. Okay a lot of help. None of it would have been possible without Jillian.

His gaze met hers. "Thank you."

JILLIAN WISHED SHE could help Avery buy the Crooked S Ranch.

She'd thought about it last evening and again this morning, but she still had no suggestions for him. A man who loved cowboying, animals, and the great outdoors definitely deserved his own ranch.

Jillian could understand that sort of passion. She'd loved making jewelry since she was a kid. She had all of those jewelry-making kits. There were the braided bracelets. The million bead sets. And her favorite, the shape-it and bake-it jewelry. For years and years, her dream was to have her own jewelry shop. And now her dream had come true. But for Avery, he had the agony of being so close and yet so far from his dream.

Knock. Knock. Knock.

The rapid knocking drew Jillian from her thoughts. Only one person knocked like that—her mother when she was in a rush. Jillian hoped her mother didn't want her to babysit Romeo that evening. She loved the little guy, but he was a handful. He was definitely not the mellow lap cat she'd imagined she was getting when she'd spotted him at the shelter.

"Come in." Jillian called out from where she was pouring her second cup of coffee.

"Was that Avery I saw at your place last night?" her mother asked, dispensing with any friendly morning greeting.

Jillian wasn't sure how to take her mother's directness. "Yes, it was."

Her mother's frown deepened. "What was he doing here?"

Jillian suddenly felt like she was twelve again and was about to be grounded. "Since when do you dislike Avery?"

"Since you sat around for six years waiting for him and then nothing. He used you as long as he needed you and then he discarded you."

Her mother had never been this vocal about her feelings for Avery. And Jillian didn't know whether to be touched that her mother cared so much for her well-being or angry that her mother was making it seem like Avery had done something wrong when in fact, he hadn't done a thing to warrant this hostility. He'd never once led her on. She'd gotten her hopes up all on her own.

"Mother, we talked about this before. He never did anything to lead me on. I liked him. He just didn't see me that way."

"But he let it go on—"

"He did no such thing. I worked as the nanny when he was working on the ranch or out of town. End of story. So give the guy some slack."

"I just don't want to see you hurt again."

"I promise, I won't get hurt. I'm long over Mr. Avery Wainwright."

Her mother's eyes said she didn't believe her, but her mother nodded just the same. "So have you found a date for the wedding?"

"Would you like some coffee?" There was just enough left in the pot for another mugful.

"No, thank you. I already had some and too much makes me jittery. Now, stop stalling. Did you find a date? Or should I call one of my friends?"

Oh boy, this is where things were going to get sticky.

Jillian considered putting it off, but she knew it was best just to put it out there. Maybe her mother would be able to vent and get it out of her system before the wedding this weekend.

Jillian took a sip of coffee. "Actually, I do have a date."

Her mother's face lit up. "That's wonderful. Who is it?"

Jillian took another sip of coffee. "It's Avery."

Her mother's smile fell. "Jillian, why would you ask him?"

"Because it made sense. I don't want a boyfriend and he doesn't want a relationship. We're going as friends. He's nothing more than my plus one."

Her mother shook her head as though none of this made any sense to her. "If that's what you believe, then you're more foolish than I ever imagined. You two will never just be friends."

And with that ominous statement, her mother turned and headed for the door. Her mother didn't even say goodbye. Instead, there was the resounding thud of the door as it swung shut.

What in the world had gotten into her mother? She always made a point of trying to get along with everyone. She acted as though Avery had walked out on Jillian on their wedding day. And that was so far from the truth.

Her mother was wrong; she and Avery could be just friends.

And then Jillian's thoughts rolled back to that moment

in her kitchen when she'd been brushing the flour from his chest. Something had happened there. It was in the way he'd looked at her. The way he touched her hand. It was as though the ground had moved beneath them.

Or it could just be her overactive imagination. It was the simplest and safest explanation. To fall for that cowboy all over again would only end one way—with her broken heart. Because his boots were made for walking...right out of Marietta. He made that known to everyone—including her. Not even the chance to own the Crooked S Ranch was going to sway him to settle down in a relationship.

Chapter Twelve

MAYBE MY MOTHER was right.

Wait. Had she just voluntarily admitted that her mother was right about her and Avery? Jillian inwardly groaned.

Avery leaned her way. "Did you say something?"

Oops! She'd have to work harder to keep her thoughts to herself. "No. It wasn't me."

Avery leaned back in his chair at Jillian's cousin's wedding. They were seated at a round dinner table with white linens. A cupcake stand in the center held eight cupcakes decorated in purple and white.

Avery had been a perfect gentleman for the past couple of hours, but he'd also been incredibly quiet. She knew he was anxious to leave. So was she.

She turned her head his way. "We're almost out of here. Just as soon as they cut the cake."

He nodded in understanding, but he still didn't say anything.

"Hello, Jillian," said a voice from behind her.

Jillian shifted in her chair to find her oldest cousin, Mary, standing there. Her husband, a named partner in a law firm, stood next to her. The man wore a frown as though his face was permanently glued into that position. His gaze never met Jillian's. She never did understand his uppity attitude toward her family, but she did her best to ignore it.

A fake smile lit up Mary's face. "Beautiful wedding, huh?"

"Yes, it is," Jillian said. "The bride and groom look so happy together."

"Now, you're the only spinster in the family." Mary wore a smug expression as she slipped her arm through her husband's.

Mary was right. With Jillian's cousin, Karen, now married, Jillian was the last of her mother's side of the family to be single. Normally this didn't bother Jillian, but sitting next to Avery, it made her wonder just how pathetic she must appear to him.

"She isn't alone." Avery turned to Mary and then he reached out for Jillian's hand. "We're together."

Mary's eyes narrowed. "I thought you were nothing more than a plus one—someone to keep Jillian from looking so—lonely."

Jillian's whole body tensed as she struggled to keep her mouth shut for her mother's sake.

Avery came to her defense. "You heard wrong," he quipped. Then he turned to Jillian. "Would you like to dance?"

Stunned into utter silence, Jillian merely nodded.

Hand-in-hand they moved away from her sputtering and fuming cousin. Jillian was still trying to wrap her mind around what had happened when Avery led her onto the dance floor.

Suddenly Jillian remembered his injured leg. "We can't dance."

His brows drew together. "Why not?"

"Your leg. I don't want to do anything to make it worse."

"I might not be Fred Astaire, but I'm healing. I don't think a little dancing will hurt."

"You're sure?"

"Positive. Now come here." He held his arms out to her.

This wasn't a good idea. But her body betrayed her and gravitated toward him. His arms were bands of muscles from his years of manual labor. His skin was permanently tanned from his days on horseback. And as he drew her close, she caught a whiff of his woodsy scent. She inhaled deeper and suppressed a sigh.

She wanted to ask what had come over him, but the other part of her didn't want to ruin this moment. Her brain had turned to mush and her heart was doing a happy tap dance in her chest. For this moment, she was going to enjoy herself. And as they made their way around the dance floor, she caught the scowl on her cousin's face. Jillian reminded herself that Mary's bad attitude wasn't her problem.

Jillian tilted her chin upward until her gaze met Avery's. "Thank you."

"I didn't do much," he said modestly.

"Oh yes, you did. I don't think anyone has ever made my cousin speechless before."

"Has she always treated you like that?"

Jillian thought back, trying to recall a time when they got along. There wasn't one memory that popped out in her mind—not as children and definitely not as adults. "I guess so. She always had to have the best. She always had to be the best. My mother blamed Mary's attitude on her being spoiled as a child. I never wasted time thinking about it."

"Something tells me she'll never be content. Instead she'll always be chasing after something bigger and better."

Not wanting to squander this moment in his arms, Jillian changed the subject. "And how about you? Have you figured out what will make you happy?"

His gaze met hers. "I'm starting to get an idea."

"Oh good. So you've figured out a way to buy the ranch?"

"Whoa! Slow down. I didn't say that."

"But you were going to. Come on, say it. Don't keep me in suspense."

He arched a brow. "Why do you care so much?"

She shrugged. "I just hate to see people give up on their dreams."

"Is that all?"

"That's all."

"Well, I hate to disappoint you, but I applied to a few online banks and they turned me down too."

"Don't worry. Where there's a will, there's a way."

He smiled at her, making her stomach somersault. "You seem awfully optimistic."

"I am."

"Seriously? Why are you so invested in me buying the ranch?"

"I just want you to be happy."

"Even if my being happy means living out on the road, moving from town to town while risking life and limb on an ornery bronc?"

She was over him. It shouldn't matter to her where he hung his cowboy hat. "Yes, even then."

This conversation reminded her of all the reasons she'd put Avery Wainwright in her rearview mirror. He was a loner and didn't stick around long enough to cool his heels. She hated that he was giving up so easily on buying the ranch.

She pulled back just a little. Avery gave her a puzzled look, but she ignored it. She needed to think clearly and being so close to him skewed her thoughts.

IT WASN'T SO bad after all.

At first, Avery was referring to the improvement with his

leg. It appeared the damage wasn't as severe as everyone had first suspected. Thank goodness.

But then his thoughts turned to this wedding and being Jillian's escort. The longer they danced and the closer he held her in his arms, the faster his heart raced.

Jillian was always beautiful, but tonight she was a knock-out. Maybe it was the peach dress with the short skirt and the teasing neckline. Or perhaps it was the way she had her blond hair pinned up with just wisps fringing her face. Whatever it was, he couldn't take his eyes off her.

That had never happened to him before. Sure he'd had his share of women pass through his life including a number of buckle bunnies, but none of them had turned his head. Tonight, Jillian had definitely turned his head. And he would love to have a casual fling with her, but there was nothing casual about Jillian. She was all about the flowers and romance, the dinner and starlight, the happily-ever-after kind of girl. She was the type of woman he'd gone out of his way to avoid.

Until now...

Attending this wedding with Jillian on his arm had him reconsidering his options. His gaze met hers. Perhaps he should roll the dice again and see what happened.

But could he ever be the man she wanted? The man she deserved?

He tried to imagine himself waking up each morning with Jillian in his arms. That wasn't hard to imagine at all. In fact, that would be the easy part.

It wasn't until he added in the baby that things got complicated. Diapers led to school and homework. Not to mention the car pools and the challenging teen years—

Jillian stopped dancing, jerking him from his musings.

He continued to hold her. "Why did you stop?"

"Because the music ended."

He stood still and listened. There was nothing but the murmur of voices. The song had in fact ended. He glanced toward the live band who were setting aside their instruments. And so his excuse to hold her in his arms had come to an end.

Avery reluctantly let her go. And then he presented his arm to escort her from the dance floor. He was still considering the tsunami of unexpected emotions that he'd experienced out on the dance floor.

Jillian stopped in her tracks and turned to him. "I think we should call it a night."

"Now? But what about the cake?"

"I…I changed my mind."

"If you're sure—"

"I am."

It was just then that he heard them call out for all of the single ladies to line up for the bouquet toss.

A worried look flickered across Jillian's face. "We have to hurry."

He couldn't help but smile as she took him by the hand

and led him to the coat check. He wondered why she was rushing away when she was the one who wanted to marry and have a baby.

Jillian was moving quickly, weaving her way through the crowd of well-wishers. He had to admit that he'd never seen Jillian run away from anything. So what or who had her moving so fast?

It wasn't until they were outside and alone that he reached out for her hand. "Hey, slow down. There's no one out here but you and me."

"I just want to go."

Snowflakes gently fell, adorning her hair. And then a flake landed on the tip of her nose before it melted. The street lamp made her eyes twinkle. His gaze dipped to her lips that were glossy and just perfect for kissing.

Without pausing to consider the ramifications of his next move, he reached out and pulled her to him. He leaned forward and claimed her lips. At first, she didn't move as though stunned by his action. He lassoed his desire, not wanting to move too fast and scare her away.

Her lips were warm and soft. He moved slowly and hesitantly.

And soon she greeted his kiss with an eagerness of her own.

Her arms slipped up over his shoulders as his hands wrapped around her slender waist. He pulled her closer. At the same time, her fingers combed through his hair.

His heart thump-thumped, harder and faster. Jillian was so beautiful, both inside and out. And her kisses were as sweet as berry pie.

He never wanted this moment to end. It was as though he'd been waiting for it all of his life—as though he'd been waiting for Jillian. And she'd been right there in front of him all of this time, but it had never been right until now.

What would she say if he proposed they explore this new facet of their relationship? He couldn't offer her any more than this magical moment, but maybe it would be enough. As she kissed him back with growing desire, his hope swelled.

Just as he was about to ask if she wanted to go back to his place, the door behind them opened. The sounds of voices made their way to them. Jillian jumped back like she'd been shocked back to reality.

Her eyes opened wide with surprise. "What did you do that for?"

"What?" He was so confused. "You mean the kiss?"

"Yes, I mean the kiss," she said with certainty. "We agreed. You were my plus one. Nothing more."

"It felt like a lot more to me."

Her gaze narrowed. "Are you feeling all right?"

"I feel fine."

She continued to give him a puzzled look.

He couldn't help but laugh. This was the most unique reaction he'd ever received after kissing someone. Leave it to Jillian to question everything.

"How about we go home?" he suggested.

"I think that sounds like your best idea yet."

"Better than the kiss?"

"Avery, stop. This isn't funny." She frowned at him. "That kiss…it can never happen again."

Why was she fighting the obvious chemistry between them? Was she concerned because he was a sworn bachelor? Or was she still hung up on that guy he'd spotted her with outside Tangled Charms?

It didn't really matter at this point. The moment had passed them by. Perhaps it was for the best. At least for now.

As they made their way to his pickup, he searched for a neutral subject to break the tension. "So you really think I should give up the rodeo and buy the Crooked S?"

Jillian hesitated as though searching for the appropriate answer. "I think you need to do what makes you happy."

"I wish it was that easy."

She paused beside the passenger-side door. "If it was easy, you wouldn't appreciate it nearly as much."

It was in that moment he realized the truth of her words. When his parents died, he had responsibilities and bills to pay. He couldn't afford to chase his dreams—literally or figuratively. His parents' life insurance was significantly less than he'd imagined. But somehow he'd managed to keep it all together.

It hadn't been easy, but he was proud of the job he'd done caring for his brother and sister. Even with the trauma of their parents' deaths, Jordan and Beth were two amazing young people. The fact he'd played a part in that made him proud.

Now, if he could summon all of that ingenuity and determination, he'd have a real shot at making his dreams come true. And he was beginning to think there was more to his dreams than he'd originally thought.

His gaze settled on Jillian. But was the thought of starting anything with her a mistake when they ultimately wanted different things in life?

Chapter Thirteen

L ESSON NUMBER TWO was about to commence.

Monday had slipped by in the blink of an eye. Avery had been busy all day. This time it didn't involve finishing the kitchen remodel. It was something far more important. With renewed vigor, he'd been on the phone with sponsors who'd shown an interest in him in the past. There had to be a way to raise the money to purchase the ranch.

Some of his contacts let his call pass to their voicemail. Some took his call and gave him a very blunt response—unless he could make a miraculous comeback on the rodeo circuit, they couldn't help him. But there were a couple who promised to look into things and get back to him. Nothing concrete, but there was at least a glimmer of hope.

For now, he had to set aside the finances because it was time for his next baking lesson.

Jillian volunteered the use of her kitchen again since his was still under construction. And she'd mentioned working on a special project for the fundraiser. She cleared off the counter next to the stove for him before she settled at the breakfast nook to work on her jewelry.

Avery straightened and closed the fridge. "You're out of eggs."

She snapped her fingers. "I knew there was something I needed to pick up on the way home." Her gaze met his. "Is that why you're frowning?"

He didn't know he was frowning. He did his best to change his expression to something more neutral, but he was obviously unsuccessful as Jillian continued to study him.

"You know," she said, "you've been wearing that glum expression since you got here. If you're not up for a lesson tonight, we can put it off until tomorrow."

He shook his head. "I don't have time to waste." He grabbed a saucepan from under the counter and placed it on the stove before adding the appropriate amount of butter. "The first round is this Saturday and I want to be prepared. So I'll caramelize the butter and then let it cool while I run to the store."

"So if it's not the lesson or the fact that I forgot the eggs, what's bothering you?"

He really didn't want to tell her, because he didn't want her to look at him differently. Although, it would feel good to talk with someone—someone he trusted. Jillian had always been there when he had problems with the kids and she'd been discreet. Avery hadn't realized it until now, but he just took it for granted that Jillian would always be there for him. Now, this was his chance to recapture that closeness.

"Avery, what is it?"

"It's the ranch." He stopped. Words like failed, rejected, and turned down stuck in his throat. Jillian would think less of him if he admitted the truth to her.

"What about the ranch?" Her eyes lit up with interest. "Have you been working on the financing for it?"

He nodded as he turned his gaze back to the butter that was now melted. He grabbed a plastic spoon from the crock next to the stove.

"Not plastic," Jillian warned. "It'll melt. Try the drawer to your left. There should be metal spoons in there."

He did as she instructed. It was so much easier to concentrate on baking rather than admitting to his failure. He just didn't want to see the disappointment reflected in her eyes.

Her voice lowered to a soft, comforting tone. "I take it things aren't going well?"

He swallowed hard. "You know that the banks turned me down." When she nodded, he continued. "So I tried some of the rodeo sponsors. Even though I was last year's champion, they want this year's leader. And thanks to my injury, it's thrown me too far back in the rankings to ever make it to the top again this season."

"Well, there has to be another way to raise the money."

"None that I can think of." And he'd spent every wakeful moment considering all plausible solutions, but none of them held up.

"Don't give up. I know how important this is to you. Sometimes it takes a lot of patience and a heap of faith to see dreams through to fruition."

"Is that what you did in order to open Tangled Charms?"

She nodded. "It is. There were a lot of times when I didn't see any way to make my dream a reality. The bank didn't want to issue me a line of credit and the owner of the building already had an interested party. The list of problems went on and on."

He knew where she was headed with this. "But you didn't give up."

"Exactly." She glanced at the pan. "Keep stirring or the butter will burn."

Jillian continued to tell him what she'd overcome to make Tangled Charms a reality. It amazed him how many hoops she'd had to jump through in order to open her own business. His own journey was beginning to look less daunting. Perhaps there were some other online resources he could try. Or maybe he could take on a partner like Jillian had done.

"Thanks for the advice." He glanced at her.

"I don't know that I would call it advice. But I hope it helps." She smiled and a warmth grew in his chest. "I have a feeling this is all going to work out."

Maybe he should adopt a bit of her optimism. What would it hurt?

A few minutes later, he pulled the caramelized butter from the stove and placed it a cold water bath. "While that cools, I'm going to get the eggs."

"Don't do that. It's my fault. I'll go." She started to get up from where she was working on a sketch of a jewelry design.

"Stay. This is my project. I'll do it." He grabbed his jacket and slipped it on. "Is there anything else you need?"

"Not that I can think of."

"I'll be right back." He grabbed his keys and headed for the door.

No matter how this Bake-Off turned out, he was going to have to figure out some special way to pay Jillian back for her generosity. She was a very special lady. Too bad he hadn't let down his guard sooner—when she was still interested in him.

KNOCK. KNOCK.

That was funny. Jillian thought Avery should still be at the store. Perhaps he forgot something. But why was he knocking when he was welcome to just walk in?

She rushed over to the door and flung it open. "Hey, I was just thinking—"

The words died in her throat. It wasn't Avery standing there. It was Glenn. What was he doing here?

The smile slipped from his face. "I take it I'm not who you were expecting."

"I…uh, Glenn, why are you here?"

He stepped past her into the apartment without an invitation, sending the door closed behind him. "Did you get my roses?"

That was it? He was upset that she hadn't called him and gushed about the roses? That would have happened if they were on good terms, but they were far from that.

"I got them, but I don't know why you sent them."

The expression on his face softened. "I told you I made a mistake." And then he moved his arm from behind his back. He was holding a bouquet of white and red carnations. "I saw these and thought of you. I had to get them." When she didn't move to accept them, he said, "Go ahead. Take them."

"I don't want them." Her voice was firm. He had no chance with her. "We're over."

His face creased with frown lines. "Why do you always have to be so difficult? This is why we broke up. Why can't you just forgive me? After all, we wouldn't have broken up if it weren't for you."

"Me?" Was he serious? It would be so easy to engage in an argument with him, but she refused to fall for his bait. He just wasn't worth getting worked up over.

He nodded. "You're just so stubborn. But I'm willing to forgive you. We can work this out."

She opened the door. "It's time you go."

He moved to place the flowers on the kitchen counter. He turned for the door and then paused in front of her. "I know you're angry now, but think about it. We're perfect together. You'll never find anyone who treats you as good as I do."

Before she could close her gaping mouth and formulate a response, he was gone. That man had some nerve. She sent the door shut with a resounding thud. Why was he suddenly so interested in getting her back? Was he that oblivious to the fact she didn't want him back? Not now. Not ever.

JILLIAN HAD COMPANY?

Avery didn't recognize the upscale SUV sitting in the driveway when he returned to Jillian's house. He couldn't imagine Jillian would invite over one of her friends when they were in the middle of a baking lesson. He glanced toward Jillian's mother's house. The lights were on, so he assumed it was her guest.

He alighted from his pickup and leaned back inside to grab the bag containing the eggs and some snacks he recalled Jillian enjoying. It was then he heard approaching footsteps. He straightened and turned.

The man approaching him was the same man he'd seen kissing Jillian on the sidewalk the other day. But Jillian had told him she didn't have a boyfriend. So what was this guy doing here?

"You must be Avery," the man, wearing a dark suit with a wool overcoat and shiny dress shoes, said. The man oozed ego and money.

"I am." Avery responded curtly. It was obvious the man had something on his mind.

The man's eyes narrowed in on him. "You need to stay away from Jillian."

Every muscle in Avery's body tensed. "That's not what Jillian wants."

A muscle in the man's cheek twitched. "I know she's upset with me right now, but we will work things out. I already picked up the pieces after you broke her heart once. Don't try it again."

He broke Jillian's heart? How was that possible? He'd never led her on. Not once. He'd made sure of it. But he had a feeling this man hadn't been so cautious with Jillian's feelings.

Avery leveled his shoulders and stared straight into the man's eyes. "I'll leave when Jillian asks me to."

"You'll regret this. Jillian is mine." The man strode away and climbed in his vehicle.

Jillian was his?

Really? Since when did Jillian become some sort of possession? No one could own her. She was a strong woman, capable of fending for herself. Avery just hoped she never bought into this man's warped thoughts.

Avery stood there until the man peeled off into the night. The thought of sweet and kind Jillian ending up with that jerk infuriated him. She deserved so much better.

Realizing he should check on her, he started up the walk. After a light tap of his knuckles on the door, he let himself inside. He didn't see Jillian at the breakfast nook where she'd been earlier that evening.

And then he spotted her in the kitchen. "Hey, is everything okay?"

She turned from where she had poured herself a cup of coffee. "I take it you ran into Glenn in the driveway?"

"Yep. Saw him."

"I, ah, hope he didn't bother you."

Avery was about to say something when he noticed the flowers on the counter. Apparently Jillian still had some sort of feelings for the man or she wouldn't have kept his flowers. The thought didn't sit well with him. Not at all.

"Everything is fine," he said, knowing it was anything but fine.

"You're sure?"

"Positive."

Confusion reflected in her eyes, but thankfully she let the subject go. "There's fresh coffee in the pot if you want some."

The last thing he needed right now was caffeine. He was plenty pumped up and wide awake. In that moment, he realized he wanted to fight for Jillian.

The decision didn't hit him like a bolt of lightning. Instead, it came to him gently as though he'd always known deep inside that they belonged together.

Now how would he convince Jillian?

Chapter Fourteen

IT HAD BEEN a great day.

Jillian smiled broadly Thursday afternoon. Not only had she completed the necklace and matching earrings for the fundraiser, but she had also put them up on display in her shop and five people had already bid on them. She'd set a starting amount, but it was bare minimum and she hoped people would be extra generous since all proceeds went to Harry's House.

"What has you smiling this afternoon?" Suzanna asked.

Jillian paused. She was smiling? "I don't know. I guess the week is going well."

"Anything special?"

"No. And it doesn't have to do with a guy if that's what you were thinking. It's just that the shop is doing well and so is our website. And the snow is falling—"

"Whoa. I have to stop you there. How do you equate snow to a good week?"

"Just because you don't like snow doesn't mean everyone feels the same way. I think it's pretty. I've loved it since I was a kid."

Suzanna shook her head. "I don't know how you can like something that's so cold and it makes a mess out of traffic. Oh, and it ruins my shoes if I forget my boots."

"But it's so tranquil when it falls. I just love watching the big fluffy flakes flutter to the ground. It blankets the earth in white, hiding the rough edges and smoothing things out." When Suzanna continued to shake her head in disagreement, Jillian asked, "You mean you don't like Frosty?"

"That's not fair. Frosty isn't real." Suzanna moved to the front door and squirted cleaner on the glass. "I think we're just going to have to agree to disagree on the subject of snow. So how's your student doing?"

"Why don't you ask him yourself?" Jillian pointed toward his pickup pulling up in front of Tangled Charms.

"Oh, I wonder what he wants." Suzanna grinned at her.

"I'm certain it's nothing like the thoughts going round in your mind."

Before they could continue their debate, Avery was at the door. Suzanna pushed it open and greeted him a little too jovially for Jillian's taste. He was going to think they were talking about him—they had been but she didn't want him to know it.

He stepped inside and brushed off the flakes of snow. "It's really coming down out there."

"I know. It's beautiful," Jillian said as casually as she could manage because right then her heart was beating rapidly. They hadn't seen each other yesterday. She had been busy finishing the earrings for the auction and he'd said he wanted to do some more work in his kitchen. "Did you change your mind about baking tonight?"

He shook his head. "Not unless you think the cookies weren't right—"

"I thought they were perfect," Suzanna chimed in.

Jillian sent her a dirty look. "She's right. They were delicious. You should win with them as long as you keep your eye on the butter."

"And don't burn it like I almost did the last time I tried to make them. Gotcha." He continued to stare at her. "What has you in such a good mood?"

His presence. Not that she would admit that to him. "I finished my donation to the Harry's House fundraiser."

"That's great." He smiled, making his eyes twinkle.

Her stomach did a somersault. "Would you like to see it?"

He nodded and followed her over to the display in the middle of the showroom. He stared into the lit display. "The necklace is beautiful. It would look really nice on you. Maybe you should wear it for promotional purposes."

Not that she wasn't tempted, but she would never do such a thing. "I don't think that would be a good idea."

"You must have lots of this jewelry at home."

"Actually I don't." When he arched a brow, she continued. "Everything I make is for the business. I figure one day when the business is secure, I'll work on something for myself."

"It's too bad you have to wait that long. Maybe you should make something for yourself now. You know, a reward for opening the shop."

"Maybe." It was a nice thought, but she knew she wouldn't do it. It wasn't like she had anywhere to wear it since she'd sworn off men. "I'm sure you didn't stop by to discuss jewelry. What did you need?"

"I was wondering if you were free tomorrow evening."

"Did you want to get started on the next recipe?"

"I have something else in mind. I promise no recipes will be involved."

Was he asking her for a date? She hadn't been expecting this and she didn't know what to say. Her mind told her to make any excuse possible to get out of it, but her heart was in direct contradiction.

"She's available," Suzanna interjected.

Avery smiled. "Is that right?"

Jillian stifled a groan and nodded. She had no idea what she'd just gotten herself into. "What should I wear?"

"Whatever. I just need your advice on something."

"Advice? I guess I could try. What is it?"

"You'll have to wait and see. You might want to bundle up. I'll pick you up at, say, six. We can grab some dinner at FlintWorks."

Was this really happening? Avery was asking her on a

date? But then she recalled that he mentioned something about advice. Perhaps she'd once again let her hopes get the better of her.

He quickly departed and Jillian refused to discuss it with Suzanna. She didn't need anyone else putting ideas in her head. She had enough of her own.

THERE WAS A heap of clothes on the bed.

Jillian had changed outfits five times until she settled on faded jeans and a light pink button top that Suzanna had given her for Christmas. Jillian had been saving it for a special occasion. She wore her hair straight down and she'd paid particular attention to her makeup, even adding some mascara, which she only did for special occasions.

She grabbed her white winter coat with the big faux-fur-trimmed hood, lined boots, and pink gloves. That should keep her warm and the combination didn't look bad together either. Not that she was trying to impress Avery or anything.

Knock. Knock.

He was early again. She started to rush to the door, but then slowed herself, not wanting him to think she was too eager about their plans.

When she pulled the door open, the smile slipped from her face. "Mom, what are you doing here?"

Her mother's brows drew together. "Who exactly were

you expecting?"

Busted. "Avery."

Her mother's eyes widened. "You're certainly seeing a lot of him these days. Do you think that's a good idea?"

Jillian retraced her steps away from the cold air and away from her mother's comments that had dampened her good mood. Her mother followed her, sending the door shut behind her. Jillian made a point of not arguing with her mother, but this was different. She didn't understand why her mother was always down on Avery.

Jillian turned to her mother. "Why is it that you can like Glenn but not Avery?"

"It's not a matter of liking one man more than the other." Her mother pressed her lips together and glanced away.

"Why are you so against Avery? This isn't new. You've been this way even when I worked for him. What did he ever do to you?"

"It's not what he did to me. It's what he did to you."

Jillian pressed a hand to her chest. "To me?"

Her mother nodded.

"But I don't understand. What did he do to me?"

Her mother frowned at her. "You surely don't think he didn't notice how crazy you were for him. No man is that oblivious."

Jillian had the same thoughts, but she always shoved them aside or told herself she was letting her imagination get the better of her. "So what are you saying?"

"That if you are going to let yourself get pulled back into his world, you need to know his intentions upfront."

Jillian didn't want to hear this again. She'd been telling herself that she was over him—that she had nothing to worry about.

"You're worried about nothing," Jillian told her mother in what she hoped was a reassuring tone. "I already told you, I'm over him."

Her mother sent her an I-don't-believe-you look. "Jillian, I wouldn't say this if I didn't love you. I just don't want you to set yourself up to get hurt again."

Jillian told herself that her mother was just being over-protective, but even she was having a hard time buying that story. Her mother would be the first one to cheer on this relationship if she thought it would lead to marriage. So was her mother seeing something that Jillian had missed?

DINNER WAS NICE.

Perhaps too nice when he was aiming for an evening with a little more spark.

Avery maneuvered his pickup in the direction of the Crooked S ranch. He chanced a glance over at Jillian. She'd been chatty about the Bake-Off all through dinner at FlintWorks, but now that they were alone in his vehicle, she'd grown quiet and appeared lost in her thoughts.

After all Jillian had done to help him prepare for the Bake-Off, he felt guilty for dragging her away from her work and consuming so much of her time that he'd arranged for a special surprise for her. He'd planned every detail. He just hoped he hadn't forgotten anything. But most of all, he hoped Jillian enjoyed it.

All around them was a winter wonderland. A blanket of snow covered most everything. Winter had settled in and didn't look as though it would be leaving anytime soon. Though springtime was his favorite time of the year with the warmer temperatures and everything springing to life, there was something magical about a snowy evening.

When they approached the turnoff for the Crooked S Ranch, he slowed down. He wheeled the pickup into the two ruts in the snow. He'd made arrangements with Blake a couple of days ago to have everything ready when they arrived. To his surprise, Blake was more than willing to help him out.

"Avery, what are we doing here?" Jillian turned to him.

"You'll find out very soon." As much as he wanted to speed down the lane, he had to take his time with the snow and ice.

"Why are you being so mysterious?"

He shrugged. "Why not? Don't you like surprises?"

"Sure. I like them when I know what they are."

Avery laughed. "You do know that's a contradiction, right?"

"What is?"

"Enjoying surprises only if you know what they are. If you know what it is, it's not a surprise."

"Fine. You win the debate. Just tell me what it is."

He rounded the big red barn and pulled to a stop. "See for yourself."

Jillian didn't say a word for a moment as her gaze took in the sight before them. "We're going for a sleigh ride?"

"We are."

"But I thought you needed to get my opinion about something."

Of course she'd remember that part. "I do. But you have to get in the sleigh before I ask you."

She turned a suspicious look in his direction.

"What?" And then he thought of something to tempt her. "I even remembered to bring a thermos of hot chocolate."

"You did?" Her eyes lit up. "Why didn't you say that first?"

He laughed. "I wonder what else I can get you to agree to in exchange for hot chocolate."

"You'll never know." She opened the door and hopped out. She turned back to him. "Well, come on. The horse is waiting."

He didn't have to be invited twice. He cut the truck engine and climbed out. With the keys pocketed, he followed Jillian to the sleigh. Blake was standing there waiting for them. A big grin covered his face as he handed over the reins.

"Thanks," Avery said. And then softly he added, "I owe you."

"That you do."

They climbed in the sleigh and then Avery covered Jillian with a heavy lap blanket. "Are you ready?"

She nodded, clutching the thermos. "I am now."

And then they were off, gliding over the snow. The snow muffled the sounds. And though the moon was hidden behind the clouds, it was still bright out. As they made their way through the field, Avery glanced over at Jillian. She was nestled beneath the plaid blanket and still clutching the thermos. She looked stunning. He should have brought her out here a long time ago.

"What are you smiling about?"

Jillian's voice drew him from his thoughts. "Who's smiling?"

"You are and you know it. So what's up?"

"Nothing. I'm just enjoying the evening." It was so much more than that, but he really didn't want to risk ruining this moment. He'd worked so hard to pull it together. He wanted to savor their time together.

For a while they glided along in silence. He had a particular destination in mind. It didn't have a name. It was just a spot where you could see for miles. And at night, it was like visiting a planetarium with all of the stars twinkling overhead.

"Are you warm enough?" he asked.

She nodded from inside her big, fuzzy hood. "I'm perfect. This is amazing. Do you take the sleigh out very often?"

He shook his head. "This is my first time. I usually come out here on horseback." He slowed the horse to a stop before turning to Jillian. "I wanted to do something special for you. A way to thank you. You've always been there for me and my family, whether it was helping me with the Bake-Off or being the best nanny in the whole world."

"You...you really think that?"

He'd obviously done a lousy job of communicating his thoughts in the past. He would have to do better going forward.

"I'm sorry I didn't make that clear before." He stared into her eyes. "I really appreciate everything you've done for me and my family."

His gaze dipped to her lips. They were shiny and full. And he was overwhelmed with the desire to kiss her again. So what was holding him back?

They were all alone on this snowy evening. And as he'd come to discover while he was planning this evening, it was a very romantic setting. If he were ever to have a chance with her, it would start beneath the starlit sky. But should he risk it? Should he put himself out there again?

It wasn't like he was asking her to marry him. It was a kiss—a simple, no-strings-attached kiss. It was a starting point.

He rested his arm over the back of the sleigh. His heart started to pound hard in his chest. He'd kissed a number of girls over the years on the rodeo circuit and he'd never put this much thought into it. But none of them had meant as much to him as Jillian. He leaned toward her.

Suddenly Jillian raised the thermos between them. "Hot chocolate?"

He settled back in his seat. Had he read the signs wrong? Was he that rusty where women were concerned?

She undid the lid on the thermos and poured the steamy cocoa into the plastic cup. She held it out to him. "Looks like we have to share."

He accepted the cup and took a drink. He could feel the warm liquid as it moved down his throat and settled in his stomach. It must be colder out here than he'd thought.

He handed back the empty cup. "Are you sure you're warm enough?"

She nodded. "I am. This lap blanket is super warm. Here." She adjusted the blanket so it could cover his legs too.

She was so close to him that he caught a whiff of her strawberry shampoo. His fingers itched to reach out and see if her hair was as silky smooth as it appeared.

Tempting fate once more, he moved his hand. As she leaned oh so near, smoothing out the blanket, his finger wrapped around a long blond lock of hair that had slipped out of her hood.

And then he had a most unwelcome thought—Glenn.

Avery didn't know how involved those two were, but enough that Jillian had kept the bouquet of flowers from him. And Glenn seemed intent on keeping her.

So that left Avery here poaching on another guy's girl. That was something he refused to do. When she turned a questioning gaze his way, he realized that he could no longer act on his thoughts of kissing her. And then he realized he still had her lock of hair wrapped around his finger. He immediately released it and lowered his hand to his side.

Jillian straightened. "There. Isn't that warmer?"

Oh yes, he was definitely warm now. He cleared his throat. "Um, yes. Yes, it is."

She smiled as though pleased with his answer. "Would you like some more hot cocoa?"

"Sure." He didn't want it. Not really. But it would give him something to do with his hands. He glanced up just then and noticed that the snow clouds were parting and the moon was visible. "Look at that." He pointed toward the sky.

The moonbeams lit up the earth around them, reflecting off the fresh layer of snow. It was so bright out that it was almost like daylight.

"This is so beautiful, like a postcard," Jillian said. "Thank you for sharing this spot with me."

This was his chance to convince her that she had other choices—other than Glenn. When she turned back to him, he dipped his head and caught her lips with his own. His heart was pounding so loud now that it echoed in his ears.

Her lips were smooth and warm. Desire pumped in his veins. He longed to devour her with a passionate kiss, but he used all of his restraint to move slowly.

She didn't move as though surprised by his kiss. Surely she couldn't be that surprised. Could she?

And then she pulled back. She avoided his gaze. "We shouldn't do that."

It was on the tip of his tongue to ask why and then he remembered Glenn. Was it really possible she still had deep feelings for that guy?

"Sorry." He wasn't sorry. Not really.

"I'm the one who's sorry. It's just that—"

"Don't." He couldn't bear to hear about Glenn. "I shouldn't have done it. Can we still be friends?"

"Of course."

He needed to smooth things over and not leave it at this awkward juncture. "Thank you again for helping me with the Bake-Off. I wouldn't be able to do it without you."

"I'm sure you would have managed." She handed over a fresh cup of cocoa.

"I don't think so." Having this generic conversation after what had happened between them felt so strange. But refusing to give up his newfound connection to Jillian, he continued. "I checked out the online videos and they just didn't work for me. But you've taught me a lot."

"I did?"

He nodded. "You taught me that you don't have to follow the directions exactly but you can take chances and switch things up."

She smiled broadly. "I'm glad you think I helped. I hope you'll think the same thing when we tackle the cake phase of the competition."

"Whoa! Slow up. We'll deal with the cookies first."

"Are you ready for the first round of the Bake-Off tomorrow?"

He took a drink of the cocoa, enjoying the warm, rich taste. "I guess I'm as ready as I'm ever going to be."

"Just do it like we went over in the kitchen and you'll be a shoo-in to win."

He almost choked on another mouthful of cocoa. He swallowed hard. "You are certainly a dreamer."

"No. I'm serious. I liked the changes you made to the cookie recipe."

He handed her back the empty cup. "I wouldn't have even known I could do that if it wasn't for you."

"I guess we make a good team." Jillian poured the rest of the cocoa in the cup.

This was the moment for him to vocalize the one thing that he'd come out here to say to her. "I agree. I know that after you quit working for me that our friendship...well, we didn't see each other much. I'm sorry I let the distance grow between us. I hope this time we'll not lose contact again. I enjoy our friendship. I hope you feel the same way."

She didn't say anything at first, as though she were processing his words. "I would like that."

"Good." With the cocoa all gone and the chill in the air starting to seep in, it was time to turn back. "We should get going."

"Oh. Do we have to? It's so beautiful out here."

"Blake will be waiting for us so he can secure everything for the night." Avery found himself disappointed they had to call an end to the evening. He'd enjoyed it much more than he'd ever imagined, even if the kiss hadn't ended as he'd planned. "We can do it another time."

Her eyes lit up. "Really?"

"Sure. You name the time and I'll make it happen."

With a big smile on her face, she said, "I'll hold you to it."

And so he got the sleigh turned around and they headed back toward the barn in a peaceful, friendly existence. There was something about her that drew him in. He didn't know if it was her undeniable beauty or something much deeper, like the quiet strength she exuded. But Avery couldn't help but feel he'd missed out on the opportunity of a lifetime—not just indulging in a passionate kiss beneath the moonlight but also having a chance to build a real relationship with Jillian—a chance to kiss her every day for the rest of her life.

As soon as he realized the direction of his thoughts, he halted them. Theirs was a case of bad timing. First, he was tied up learning to be the guardian of his siblings. And now

that he was free, she was involved in an on and off relationship with Glenn. Frustration balled up in Avery's gut,
dimming his good mood.

Chapter Fifteen

HERE WENT NOTHING.

Or here went everything.

It all depended on how he looked at it.

Avery's muscles were tense and his gut was wrenched into a nervous knot. He told himself not to let the event get to him. It wasn't like this was his first time performing in front of people. Every time he stepped in the arena at the rodeo, thousands of people were in attendance. He'd learned how to block them out. So why wasn't it working now?

Perhaps it was because he didn't feel confident about his baking skills. And now he had to do it from beginning to end in front of people he'd known all of his life. Talk about pressure.

Most of all, he missed Jillian being next to him. She'd claimed it was because she had to man her stall at the event. He glanced down at the black band on his wrist with Harry's House printed in white. He had been one of her first customers.

The wristbands were a good idea. He just wished he

could trade places with Jillian. He could sell the bands while she did the baking. It would have been for the best, but there was no backing out now.

He wondered if Jillian had arrived already. So many people had arrived early that it surprised him. It appeared it was going to be a sold-out crowd.

After circling the cafeteria for the second time, he neared the doorway to the kitchen. When he heard his name called out, he paused. His heart picked up its pace. Was it possible Jillian had changed her mind and would be close at hand to cheer him on?

He turned, searching for Jillian in the crowd of people. And then he spotted Joanie, Harry's younger sister, waving at him. He made his way over to her.

"I wanted to wish you good luck." She smiled. "What are you going to bake for this round?"

"Cowboy cookies with a few personalized modifications."

"Sounds intriguing. I'm sure you'll do great."

"Thanks." He glanced around, hoping to find Jillian in the crowd, but he didn't see her anywhere. "I better get inside."

"Before you run off, do you want to buy some raffle tickets?" She held up the red tickets.

"Sure. Why not?"

"How many would you like?"

He shrugged. He really didn't care about winning, he just wanted to make a donation. He pulled out his wallet and yanked out a wad of small bills, wishing he had more money on him. He'd make sure he brought more with him for the next round.

After Joanie counted out the money, she tore off the appropriate number of tickets. The tickets were paired, one for the entrant and one for the drawing later that evening. He folded his tickets and tucked them in his back pocket while Joanie placed the matching set of tickets in a box for the drawing.

He scanned the room once more, trying to find Jillian. And then he spotted her. She had set up a small stall with a banner that read: Tangled Charms supports Harry's House. On one side of the banner was the silhouette of a house and the other side had a saw and hammer crossed. It was just like the design on his wristband.

As though Jillian sensed he was staring at her, she glanced in his direction. Suddenly his worries over tonight's competition slid to the back of his mind. All he could think about was going to Jillian and making sure things were still all right between them.

He'd taken a step in Jillian's direction when Jane McCullough stepped in front of him. "Hi. I was wondering where you were."

"I just arrived."

"No problem. Your workstation is this way." She indicated the opposite direction from Jillian's stall.

"I was just going to step over there." He motioned to

Jillian, who appeared to be watching his exchange with Jane.

"I'm afraid it'll have to wait. We need to get you in your apron and set up at your station. This competition is set to start shortly." She took his arm and starting walking.

He had no choice but to follow along unless he wanted to make scene. He glanced over his shoulder, but Jillian was now distracted with some customers.

He grudgingly followed Jane into the kitchen. He hadn't been back to Marietta High School since his brother and sister had attended. And even though they'd graduated less than a year ago, it still seemed as though a lifetime had passed.

Jane walked very quickly. Luckily, his leg was actually feeling a lot better. But everyone, including his physical therapist, had warned him not to overdo it. Little did they know he was already considering heading back out on the circuit to win some money. He just had to do everything he could to buy the Crooked S like Howard would have wanted.

Jillian was more excited than she'd been expecting.

With everyone seated to watch the baking competition, there were no more customers to buy the wristbands; so Jillian had moved toward the front where she could get a good view of the bachelors. There were eight of them in total. She smiled when she realized they all looked as though they would rather be anywhere but standing in front of half of the town.

Just then Mrs. Monroe said, "Okay, bachelors, start your cookies!" Then she rang a little bell.

Everyone cheered and the baking began.

Jillian was so excited for Avery. Even if he didn't win, she was proud of him. It took a lot for him to get up there in front of everyone. She finally squeezed her way up to the front of the room. She walked by Avery's station just as he was browning the butter. He glanced her way and smiled. She could tell by the stiff smile and the worry in his eyes that he was nervous about the competition.

One of the contest coordinators stopped to ask him something just as the butter started to bubble. Jillian noticed how Avery stopped stirring. He moved away from the stove to grab a piece of paper. Oh no! She wanted to rush over and continue stirring for him. She knew from experience just how easy it was to burn the butter. But there was nothing she could do. With this being a competition, there could be no interference. But who was to say she couldn't signal him?

She moved until she was in his line of sight and then, as discreetly as she could, she motioned toward the butter. When he got her message, his eyes opened wide and he rushed back to the stove.

Jillian walked back to the craft stall that she was manning with Suzanna. She could only hope the butter was okay.

Because she knew Avery could bake these cookies—she'd sampled one, then another, followed by a few more. After all, it was her job as his mentor to make sure they were tasty.

"Well, how's it going over there?" Suzanna asked.

"I don't know."

"Oh no. That doesn't sound good."

"It's just that Avery got distracted and I'm afraid the butter burned. Hopefully I'm wrong."

"It'll be fine. You taught him well."

Jillian was surprised by how invested she was in this competition. After all, she was just an instructor, albeit a reluctant one at that. But the atmosphere of the townspeople was contagious. They were all excited about the competition and cheering everyone on. Perhaps she would have favored Avery, even if he wasn't her student.

At last, Avery pulled a tray of cookies from the oven and replaced it with a new tray. Jillian quietly watched from the sidelines as he set the timer. They'd worked hard to figure out just the right amount of time to bake them, but she'd forgotten to mention that the baking time could fluctuate with a different oven. She hoped Avery would think of that.

And now that the cookies were pulled from the oven, she waited and wondered how he did. When a small smile lifted his lips, she knew they hadn't burned. She knew he could do it.

"And now while we wait for the cookies to cool," Mrs. Monroe said, "we'll pull the ticket for the honeymoon suite at the Graff Hotel. Are you ready?"

There was a murmur of agreement that rippled through the crowd. She read off the winning ticket number. Jillian watched as everyone pulled out their tickets. She didn't have any. She had absolutely no use for a room at the Graff Hotel, much less the honeymoon suite.

Her gaze strayed back to Avery as he moved the cookies from the hot baking sheet to a cooling rack. He looked like a real pro up there. She smiled. Jillian was so happy she'd been able to help him...even if things had gotten a little complicated at times.

"So who is our winner?" Mrs. Monroe scanned the crowd but no one raised their hand. "Come on. Don't be shy. I know someone here won. Check your numbers again." She read off the lucky number again.

Still, no one raised their hand.

And then Mrs. Monroe said, "I think I have an idea." She turned to face the bachelors. "Gentlemen, I know you're all busy, but if any of you bought raffle tickets, you need to check them now."

A few men reached into their pockets and pulled out a strip of tickets. Jillian smiled, knowing one of them had won and wondering which one. But when Avery set aside the spatula and reached into his pocket, the smile faded from her face.

Please don't let it be him.

Her pulse raced. Everyone who was anyone in town was

here tonight, including her mother. If he were to win the honeymoon suite, everyone would once again think they were a couple. That at last they had worked things out and they were going to have a happily-ever-after.

But it wasn't the case. It didn't matter that when he stared at her, her stomach dipped. And when she was close to him, she couldn't resist inhaling his manly scent. And that at night, her dreams were filled with him. Because in the end, he'd told her in no uncertain terms that he didn't want another family. They had no chance for anything more than what they had now—an awkward friendship.

"What was the number again?" Avery asked.

Jillian's heart sank. She should leave, but her feet were unwilling to move. It was like watching a looming accident and not being able to turn away.

Mrs. Monroe repeated the number and with every digit Avery nodded his head.

"That's it," he said, looking pleased that he had the winning ticket.

"Wonderful!" Mrs. Monroe beamed as she rushed over and verified that it was indeed the winning ticket. "Congratulations. I bet Jillian is excited too."

Oh no! At last jarred from her stupor, she turned and slipped out a side door. She started walking down the long hallway, away from everyone. There was no way she was going to stick around for this.

How could Avery have done this? Didn't he realize what

people were going to say? Anger and embarrassment burned inside her. She headed straight for the back exit. Lucky for her, it was unlocked to let the vendors and suppliers come and go. The cold air felt good against her heated skin.

She wanted to keep going, but she couldn't. She had to return to the stall unless she found someone to fill in for her.

She reached for her phone and started texting Suzanna:

Jillian: *Something came up. Have to leave. Can you watch over the stall?*

Suzanna: *Are you feeling all right?*

Obviously Suzanna had missed the thing with the winning ticket. And then she recalled that they'd sold so many bands that Suzanna had run back to the car to get more.

Jillian: *I just got a sudden headache.*

It wasn't far from the truth. Not far at all. Right now her temples pulsed and her stomach churned. She'd be better once she got home. Hopefully by tomorrow the rumors and innuendos would die down. Jillian knew that was as likely to happen as the sun not rising tomorrow.

Suzanna: *I've got it. Go home. I'll see you tomorrow.*

Jillian got the t and h of her thank-you message typed when she heard her name being called. She glanced up to see Avery charging toward her.

"Hey, where are you going?" he asked, as though he

hadn't realized what he'd done.

"I'm leaving." She finished typing the rest of her message to Suzanna before slipping the phone in her pocket.

"You don't have to do that."

"Yes, I do. Didn't you see all of those people? Their gazes were going from you to me and back again."

"So what? You know they get excited about the slightest thing."

The slightest thing? Is that what he thought about her feelings? That they were a slight thing? Or was he totally oblivious to everything?

Just in case he really didn't understand what was at stake here, she intended to tell him. "This isn't some little bit of gossip. They think that you and I are finally a couple."

"So they're wrong."

She shook her head. "I'm not going through this again."

"Again? What's that supposed to mean?"

She was just angry enough at that moment not to be embarrassed when she admitted everything to him. "That when I used to work for you—that they all thought—that I thought—things between us were going to turn serious. The whole town was talking about it. That we made a good pair. They would ask me all the time if we were getting married."

Avery raked his fingers through his hair. "But I don't understand. You and I, we never even dated."

"You don't have to tell me. Obviously they were all wrong. Because no matter what I did, you never noticed me in that way. Even when I asked you to the Christmas Stroll."

His eyes widened. "But I couldn't. You worked for me. And—"

"It doesn't matter now."

"Of course it matters."

"I'm not doing this. I'm not dealing with the questions and assumptions again. I'm leaving." She turned and started to walk away as fast as her legs would carry her.

"Jillian, don't go. I'll fix this."

She didn't even want to know what that meant because there was no way he could fix this. Because she'd been fooling herself when she told herself that she was over him. She wasn't. Not at all. It's the reason none of her other relationships had worked out.

She was in love with a man who didn't want a future with her.

Chapter Sixteen

H E WASN'T GIVING up.

Not on purchasing the ranch. And not on Jillian.

The more time Avery spent with Jillian, the more convinced he became that there was something between them—something more than friendship. Perhaps he'd moved too fast. And winning the raffle drawing for the honeymoon suite had been the ultimate in bad luck.

At the time, he thought he'd been doing a good thing when he bought those raffle tickets. He had a history of never winning those giveaways anyway. He'd actually never even bothered to ask about the prize.

And to top it off, his mishap with the butter had cost him the first round of the Bake-Off. As it was the local vet, Matthew West, won it with his chocolate macadamia nut cookies. Avery sighed and shook his head as he sat in his pickup. He sure hoped the second round of the competition went better.

It was Monday evening, time for his prearranged baking lesson with Jillian. They'd settled on lessons three nights a week. Monday, Wednesday, and Friday. He hadn't heard from Jillian since round one of the Bake-Off. He thought of calling her to see if she still wanted to work with him, but he knew it would be too easy for her to turn him away. And if he were truthful with himself, he didn't want that. He wanted to continue with these baking lessons.

That fact surprised him. He was the one who didn't want anything to do with this Bake-Off originally and now he was looking for ways to keep going. He knew he had a competitive streak, but there was something more to this desire.

Jillian's face came to mind. She'd been so good to him. He just didn't understand how she'd jumped to the conclusion that he would do anything to hurt her. In fact, the opposite was true.

He pulled his truck up in Jillian's driveway. He was relieved to find her car there. Now he just wondered how he'd get past the front door. He thought of coming armed with flowers, but he didn't want to repeat Glenn's gesture. Instead, Avery arrived empty-handed but armed with a heartfelt apology.

He stepped up to her door and paused. He sucked in a deep breath, leveled his shoulders, and knocked. When there was no response, he knocked with a little more force.

"Coming," Jillian said.

Well, that had to be a good sign. He was half-expecting her to tell him to go away. Unless she was expecting someone else. The thought of Glenn came to mind. Avery's jaw tensed.

The door swung open. Jillian stood there in jeans and a red top that clung to all of her amazing curves. Her hair was pulled back in a ponytail. She wasn't smiling, but at least she hadn't slammed the door in his face.

"Well, don't stand out there. Come in. It's cold out."

He stepped inside. "You look nice. Were you expecting someone else?"

He braced himself for her answer. The memory of Glenn claiming that Jillian was his girlfriend came to mind. Avery had hoped she would see through that man's charade. He wasn't good for her and if Avery could tell that within a couple of minutes of meeting him, he didn't want to imagine the damage Glenn could do to Jillian's life if given enough time.

She laced her fingers together. "No. Well, yes. You. We need to talk."

Oh no. He knew that tone. He was in trouble. "Listen, about the raffle. I'm sorry. I didn't know what the tickets were for. I thought I was just making a donation. I never thought I'd win. I didn't want to win. I just wanted to make a contribution to Harry's House."

Jillian waved off his explanation. "You don't have to apologize. But I do. I overreacted."

What? Had he heard her correctly? She was apologizing?

She moved into the living room and sat down on the chair. "I thought I had put everything in the past—the rumors about us—the expectations that we'd get married—all of it. You know how small this town is. And I'm sure you couldn't avoid all of the gossip while I was working for you. Everyone thought we were the up-and-coming 'it' couple."

He'd ignored it at the time. It had been so much easier. He'd had so many responsibilities back then that he couldn't take on any more. But he couldn't lie to Jillian. And he couldn't hide from the truth any longer.

"I heard the rumors. But I ignored them and figured the people repeating them had too much time on their hands."

"And now they are talking again." Jillian frowned.

"Because I won the honeymoon suite?"

Jillian nodded. "That and because we're spending so much time together."

Avery's thoughts turned to her relationship with Glenn. Avery was certain Glenn wouldn't have been happy about the raffle win or the gossip. Avery considered inquiring about him but decided he wouldn't like the answer. After all, Glenn appeared to be well enough off by the looks of his clothes and the car. He could offer Jillian a good life. And if Avery couldn't purchase the ranch, he wouldn't have anything to offer Jillian. He'd be heading back out on the rodeo circuit.

Avery gave some consideration as to how best to handle this situation. He could only come up with one answer and he didn't like it. "I don't want to cause you more problems. I'll be going."

"No. Don't. You can stay."

"I think it's better that I go. This way the gossip will die down. I never meant for anything like this to happen. I don't want anyone to get the wrong idea and make this worse for you." He just couldn't bring himself to mention Glenn's name.

"I mean it. Stay. I shouldn't let what people say bother me so much."

He was torn between staying and going. But when he looked into her eyes and saw the open honesty in them, his decision was made. "Then we better get to work. I don't know anything about making a caramel apple pie except that I enjoy eating it."

So they set to work. Once the apples were peeled, cored, and soaking, they got to work on the crust. He quickly learned there were only a handful of ingredients: butter, flour, salt, and water. It sure seemed simple enough, at the time.

With Jillian working next to him, he watched as she cut the butter into the flour and salt. He did the same until the mixture resembled coarse crumbs. And then they added the icy cold water, a tablespoon at a time until the dough formed a smooth ball.

He smiled at Jillian. "I think I've got it."

"Now for the next important step, rolling out the dough for the crust."

Okay. He had no idea what that entailed. But Jillian had

thought ahead and borrowed her mother's rolling pin so she could show him what to do. She went first and explained everything she was doing and then he tried it.

It took a few tries to get the rolling motion down. He spent a lot of time making the dough even. But when he went to lift it, the middle was completely stuck to the counter.

"Oh no," Jillian said. "You don't have enough flour on the counter to keep it from sticking."

He gathered the dough, cleaned the counter, spread a liberal amount of flour over the counter, and tried again. He'd keep trying like he had with the cookies until he got it. And this time he wouldn't let himself get distracted at the competition like he had with the butter and let it burn. When the two pies were assembled, they slid them in the oven. Avery breathed a sigh of relief.

By the time the pies came out of the oven, the dishes were washed up and he was getting tired. Who knew that baking could be such hard work?

"Well, now that those are done, I should get out of your way," he said.

"They aren't done."

"They aren't?"

She shook her head. "Well, the pie is but you aren't. This is a baking competition so you're going to want to make the top of the pie as appealing as possible. We'll work on making a lattice top when you come over for your next lesson on

Wednesday."

He swallowed hard. "I have to make it pretty too?"

She smiled and nodded. "It is a competition."

"But I thought pie was served with a scoop of ice cream on top."

"Yes, you can do it that way. Or you can slice the pie carefully and let your hard work speak for itself by not hiding it under the ice cream."

"All right. You're the boss."

She shook her head. "Not the boss. Just the mentor. In the end, it's your pie to do as you see fit."

At this point, he said good night. This evening had gone far better than he'd hoped. It made him optimistic for the future—their future. But before he could make a serious play for Jillian, he needed to have his life sorted.

His thoughts drifted back to buying the ranch. He'd given the idea of taking on a partner some serious thought. It couldn't be just anyone. Time and again, he thought of Blake, who respected the land and animals like he did.

Chapter Seventeen

S HE COULDN'T GET behind. Not today.

Wednesday afternoon arrived quickly. Jillian had been pushing herself all day to stay on top of things. There were emails to answer, supply orders to place, and a special order necklace to make. It all had to be completed by the end of the day. And she couldn't fall behind.

Tonight was her next baking lesson with Avery. And not only did they have to go over making a decorative pie top, but she also had to show him how to finish it with a caramel glaze. She would have to see if she could find a fluted pastry cutter on the way home. A lattice top for this type of pie was risky since it was unusual, but she felt it would really set it apart.

Suzanna glanced up from where she was working on a new figurine. "And what has you smiling?"

"Nothing in particular."

"Uh-huh. I've never seen you smile like that for me."

Jillian schooled her features into a serious expression, even though inside she was still smiling. "Who says that I'm smiling about someone?"

"I do. I've known you since we were in kindergarten. And something is up, so out with it."

"It's no big deal." That was a lie. It was a great big deal. "I've decided that I've let the town's gossip dictate too much of my life and from now on I'm doing what I please with whom I please and they can say whatever they want."

Suzanna smiled. "Well, it's about time."

"What's that supposed to mean?"

"That I've watched you over the years shy away from things you want because you're afraid that it'll upset your mother or get the gossips started. As one person who has recently been the highlight of the town gossip, I can tell you that what they say means nothing. Most of the time they have their facts all wrong."

Jillian remembered everything Suzanna had to endure after she got stood up at the altar. That had been such a tragic time in Suzanna's life. It was still only less than a year ago, but Suzanna seemed to have worked through most of it, although she was still leery of dating.

"I'm sorry you had to go through all of that," Jillian said.

Suzanna shrugged. "I guess it could have been worse."

"How's that?"

"He could have married me."

"That's true." Jillian couldn't imagine getting married to someone who didn't love her back. "I'm sure you'll find a really great guy who will deserve you and treat you like a queen."

Suzanna laughed. "I don't know about that. First, we have to get you all situated."

"Situated? What's that supposed to mean?"

"It means you have two men fighting for your attention. You need to pick one."

She shook her head. "There's no one to pick."

"So you like them fighting over you?"

"What are you talking about? I told Glenn to leave me alone. As for Avery, we're just friends."

Suzanna got an oh-no-I-said-too-much look on her face. "I should get back to work."

"Oh no, you shouldn't. What did you mean about Avery and Glenn fighting over me?"

"I...I thought you knew." Suzanna picked up a sculpting tool and made an adjustment to the figurine of a little boy with a baseball cap. "I shouldn't say anything. It was gossip anyway. And you just said that you weren't going to pay attention to gossip."

"This is different. If there's something I should know, you have to tell me."

Suzanna sighed and placed her tool on the table. She leaned back in her chair as her gaze moved to the empty doorway. "Okay. Carol Bingley heard this from Gloria Weaver who heard it from Jane Farr who heard it from your next door neighbor that last week there was a confrontation in your driveway between Avery and Glenn."

"I knew they'd run into each other, but as far as I know they didn't actually have a conversation."

"That's not what your neighbor said. She heard Glenn threaten Avery to stay away from you because you two were getting back together."

"Really? Funny, Avery didn't mention it." Just then the phone rang and since it was sitting closest to Jillian, she said, "I'll get it." Jillian rushed over to the phone. "Tangled Charms. May I help you?"

"Yes," said a male voice. "I would like to speak with a Jillian Parker."

"Speaking." She wondered if someone had picked up her business card at the Bake-Off and was interested in a special order. That would be wonderful. "What can I do for you?"

"I need to set up a time for you to come in and sign the final paperwork."

"Paperwork? Who is this?" Warning bells were going off in Jillian's head.

"My apologies. My name is Stan Hansen. I'm with the Crawford Savings & Loan in Bozeman. I have the paperwork you submitted, and to approve the loan, we need you to come in—"

"Loan? What loan? Does this have something to do with Tangled Charms?" She'd done all of the financial business with the local bank. Was it possible they sold her small business loan? If so, would they have done it so soon?

"Uh, yes, it does have to do with Tangled Charms." Mr.

Hansen now sounded as confused as she did. "You agreed to put up your business to secure a loan for Mr. Glenn White."

"I did no such thing!" Her voice was louder than she'd intended, but she was furious. And she didn't care that Suzanna had stopped working and was now moving toward her. "I would never do such a thing."

"But I have your signature right here."

"I'm sorry, but you've been lied to. That is not my signature."

There was silence on the other end of the phone. "Are you saying that fraud has been committed?"

Jillian hesitated. Fraud sounded so severe. But then again, so was trying to leverage her business—her dream—out from under her. And it wasn't just hers, it was Suzanna's too.

"Yes, I am."

"Okay. I will be in contact shortly."

Jillian hung up and immediately went in search of her cell phone because she didn't know Glenn's number by heart.

"What's going on?" Suzanna had a concerned look on her face.

Jillian placed the call, but after three rings it went to Glenn's voicemail. "I know what you did and you aren't going to get away with it."

For the first time since opening the shop, Jillian was relieved that they had no customers. When she set her phone aside, she realized her hands were shaking from the fury pumping through her veins. She took a deep breath and then repeated to Suzanna everything that had just transpired.

"I can't believe it." Suzanna's face was red with anger. "I knew I didn't like that man and now I have a really good reason. What do you think will happen?"

"I don't know. But whatever it is, he brought it on himself."

Suzanna's mouth gaped and her eyes widened. "This must be why he came crawling back and was trying to win you over. It's a good thing you didn't fall for anything he said."

Jillian's stomach churned at the thought of him thinking he could use her like that. In that moment, her faith in her judgment in men diminished.

Chapter Eighteen

JILLIAN SAT AT the worktable behind the counter of Tangled Charms. Suzanna was out at the post office, shipping various packages for the online portion of their business before she went to pick up some supplies.

The shop was void of customers, giving Jillian a moment to enjoy the quiet. As she worked on a new piece of jewelry, her mind shifted to the fundraiser. She smiled, thinking of how the wristbands had been a big hit and the necklace already had a number of blind bids. Between the two of them, she'd be able to make a respectable contribution to the cause.

And then she came to a delicate part of the necklace. All of her concentration was focused on connecting these two S-shaped pieces of the necklace. She pulled her bottom lip between her teeth as the tension mounted. There were small S-shaped curls linked with larger S-shaped curls. The way they were attached gave them the freedom to move. She just had to loop this piece of metal ever so carefully through—

The bell above the door jangled.

Jillian jumped.

Why, oh why, did they have to pick that moment to enter the store? She suppressed a frustrated sigh, set the necklace aside, and stood up to greet the customer. Jillian glanced up and found Beth Wainwright standing just inside the door, looking around at the shop. Immediately, Jillian's frustration melted away. It was replaced with a big smile.

Jillian rushed out from behind the counter. "Beth, I didn't know you were in town."

"I just got here."

They hugged.

Jillian pulled back. "What brought you home?"

"I didn't have any Friday classes, so I thought I'd drive home and check out the Bake-Off tomorrow."

"I think you'll be pleasantly surprised." Jillian recalled the delicious apple pie that Avery had baked all on his own.

"Thank you so much for helping him. I've been worried about him since this latest accident. I wish he'd give up the rodeo. He's not as young as he used to be."

Jillian suppressed a laugh. Since when did twenty-seven constitute old age? But she supposed to an eighteen-year-old it might seem that way.

"Then you must be so happy that he's seriously considering purchasing the Crooked S Ranch."

Beth's eyes momentarily widened. "Um, yes, I am. How's that going?"

Jillian didn't see how it would hurt anything to update

Beth since she already knew about Avery's plans. Jillian was sure he'd give his sister the details later.

"I don't know much. I just know that the bank won't give him the loan until he comes up with more cash and he hasn't had any luck with any sponsor spots. But he hasn't given up. He'll find a way to make it work." Jillian moved to the coffee maker that they'd decided to put in the front of the shop for visitors. She picked up a cup and held it out to Beth. "Would you like some?"

Beth nodded. "Thanks." She paused as though thinking over what Jillian had just told her. "How much more does he need?"

"I don't know. I'm sure when you catch up with him he'll fill you in on the details."

"He should sell the house."

That statement had Jillian spilling coffee over the edge of the mug. She reached for a napkin to clean up the small mess.

After Jillian wiped up the drops of coffee, she straightened. "Your brother would never do that. It's your home. He's been working very hard to fix it up."

"I'm serious. He should sell it. Then he could roll that money into the ranch."

Jillian got the distinct feeling that Beth was totally serious. "But the house doesn't belong solely to him, does it?"

"Maybe not legally but as far as Jordan and I are concerned, it's his. I know it's hard for Avery to accept, but

Jordan is making his career in the Air Force. And I have plans that don't include Marietta. Our home is wherever my brother is. The memories we already have tucked in our hearts. No sale could ever take those away from us."

Jillian was deeply touched by the love between these siblings. "Sounds like you should be talking to Avery."

"I would but he never hears me. He still treats me like I'm ten. But I have another idea in mind to show him just what I mean."

Jillian didn't like the sounds of that. Beth did have a tendency to act first and think later. Sometimes Jillian wondered if she should be more like Beth instead of cautiously planning out her life, but she also knew that Beth got herself in a lot of messes. Maybe Jillian's cautious tendencies weren't so bad after all.

"Do you mind if I ask what you have in mind?"

Beth gave her a broad smile. "I think I have the answer for everyone." She glanced at the coffee. "Do you mind if I pass on the coffee? There's someplace I need to be."

"No problem. If you need anything, I'm here."

Beth gave her a hug. "You're already doing enough by helping my brother with the Bake-Off. Thank you so much. Now I've got to go."

And with that Beth disappeared out the door, leaving Jillian to worry about what the young woman had in mind. Her first instinct was to phone Avery and fill him in. But Beth wasn't a kid anymore. She was grown up and it wasn't

Jillian's job any longer to fill Avery in on his sister's activities. Besides, she had a feeling Avery would find out about this mysterious plan soon enough.

SO HIS LITTLE sister was home.

Avery had yet to see her, but Jillian had called to see if he wanted to cancel tonight's baking session. At first, he hadn't understood. He thought Jillian was backing out because she was washing her hands of mentoring him, but then she'd mentioned his sister. Suddenly the pieces began to fall into place.

When he rang Beth's phone, she didn't pick up. He assumed she was catching up with friends since she hadn't been home since the holidays. He had to admit that he found this spontaneous visit highly suspect. What had drawn her home when she was supposed to be wrapped up in her classwork?

He'd just concluded a meeting with Blake where he'd laid out his plans for the ranch. He'd proposed ideas of how they could co-own it. Blake had sounded interested until Avery had mentioned the financial obligations. Blake didn't waste any time making it perfectly clear he didn't have access to that kind of money.

Avery's fingers tightened on the steering wheel. Why did everything have to be so difficult?

And then Jillian's words came back to him: *If it was easy, you wouldn't appreciate it nearly as much.*

And to give up on purchasing the Crooked S meant giving up on keeping Jillian in his life as more than his friend. Because the more time they spent together, the harder it became to deny his growing feelings for her.

He knew she deserved more than a cowboy who spent his life on the road going from one rodeo to the next. She deserved someone who would be there for her day in and day out—like she'd been there for his family. He just had to buy the Crooked S. It would make them both happy.

In silence, he drove home. He couldn't stop thinking that if he tried harder there would be an answer that he'd missed. Or maybe he was just refusing to accept the inevitable.

When he drove up his road, his gaze snagged upon a For Sale sign. He was surprised to find one of his neighbors was moving. Usually he heard about these things before they happened. And then he realized the sign was sitting in his yard.

What in the world is going on?

He didn't even tap the brakes as he wheeled into the driveway. And that's when he spotted the cute little car that he'd bought his sister. He sensed she was the root of the problem, but he had no idea what she was up to. Why in the world would Beth want to sell her home?

He hopped out of the truck. A twinge of pain in his knee

didn't slow him down as he hurried up the walk. He swung the front door open. "Beth! Beth, where are you?"

She strolled out of the kitchen with Marshmallow in her arms. "Would you quit yelling? You're upsetting the cat."

He glanced at the cat who was squirming to be let loose. Beth bent over and set the cat on the floor. His gaze returned to his sister as he waited for an explanation for the sign in the yard. And then realizing that in his surprise he'd forgotten to pull the sign, he rushed back out the door.

Beth was hot on his heels. "What are you doing?"

Without a word, he strode toward the sign.

"Avery, don't you dare!" When he yanked the sign from the yard, she said, "Put it back."

He didn't care what she said. The sign was going away. If this was some sort of prank, it wasn't funny. He took the sign and marched over to the garbage can by the side of the garage. Knowing it would never fit into the can, he placed it beside it. He turned to face Beth. "Now, you have some explaining to do."

She crossed her arms and glared at him. "Not out here, it's cold."

They returned to the front porch and found they'd run outside without closing the door. Avery sighed as he followed his sister inside and closed the door. He didn't bother to mention all of the wasted heat. He had more important matters on his mind.

He drew in a deep breath and blew it out. "Why did you

put the For Sale sign in the yard? Is this some sort of joke?"

"Not at all." Beth still had her arms crossed. "And I'm putting it back."

He rubbed the back of his neck. This didn't make any sense. "Why would you want to sell your home? This is where you grew up. It's where all our memories of Mom and Dad are. How could you do this?"

"I…I'm doing it for you."

"For me?" If he was confused before, he was even more so now.

She nodded. "Jillian told me—"

"Jillian's involved in this?" He had been sharing a lot with her lately, but he never thought she would resort to conspiring with his sister.

"She told me about the Crooked S and how you need money to buy it."

How could Jillian have taken what he'd told her and repeated it to his sister? Was this what Jillian wanted? For him to buy the Crooked S at all costs?

He shook his head. "Jillian was wrong. I'm not buying the ranch. Do you hear me?"

Beth lifted her chin. "You need to let go of the past."

"And you don't need to tell me what to do. Remember, I'm the big brother here."

"Someone has to tell you when you're making the biggest mistake of your life. Jillian is never going to settle down with a cowboy who is on the rodeo circuit constantly."

"Who said I was getting serious with Jillian?" He needed to straighten this out with Jillian before there were any more misunderstandings. "I'll be back. And then we're going to talk some more."

As he headed for the door, his sister called out, "And maybe then you'll listen to reason."

Avery moved quickly to his truck. He was a man on a mission, as it seemed all of the women in his life had lost their minds. Why in the world would anyone even think of selling his parents' house?

Jillian's apartment wasn't far from his house, which didn't give him any time to cool down and think out what he was going to say. As Avery pulled in the driveway, he noticed a movement out of the corner of his eye. He turned to see the tip of a white tail going around the corner of the apartment. Romeo?

That cat was outside more than he was inside. Avery sighed. He really didn't want to go chasing after a cat. He had important matters to settle. But he couldn't just let a house cat run around in the cold.

With a sigh, he set off in pursuit of the ornery feline. "Here, kitty, kitty."

He wished he had some treats with him. Just the jiggle of the pouch should draw the cat out from whatever hiding spot he was hunkered down in.

Avery glanced around at the shrubbery, not seeing any signs of Romeo. Now where had the cat disappeared to?

Avery had searched the entire perimeter of the house when the front door swung open.

"Avery?"

"Yeah, it's me." He frowned as he glanced up in time to see a white cat dash into Jillian's apartment. Wait. That wasn't Romeo. "It's Marshmallow."

Jillian nodded. "Come on in. It's cold out there."

He followed Jillian inside, pulling the door closed behind him. He glanced into the living room area and found Marshmallow on the couch next to Romeo. How in the world had that cat known where to find Romeo? Avery was beginning to think that cats had sixth senses or some such thing.

He shook his head and turned back to Jillian—the reason for his visit.

Before he could speak, Jillian said, "It looks like Romeo has been teaching Marshmallow some of his tricks." She smiled. "Aren't they cute together?"

He glanced over at the cats who were seated side by side. Maybe in another instance he would have agreed, but right now he wasn't in the mood for cute. He turned back to Jillian to find her continuing to smile. He wished she'd quit doing that. It was hard to be angry when her face was all lit up and her eyes twinkled.

"Would you stop that?"

Her eyes widened. "Stop what?"

"Smiling like there's nothing wrong."

The smile slipped from her lips. "What's wrong?" And then she glanced back at the cats and the smile returned to her lips. "Oh, you mean Marshmallow running away. Don't worry. She looks perfectly fine. Maybe we should set up dates for these two so they quit running away from home in order to visit each other."

"Stop with the cats," he ground out. "This has nothing to do with them and you know it."

"Boy, you're in quite a mood." She walked into the kitchen. "Would you like a muffin?"

"No. I wouldn't. I want you to tell me why you talked my sister into selling our home."

Jillian's eyes widened. "I...I didn't. I had no idea."

He studied her expression, admiring the way she could so easily fake a surprised expression. "Don't play coy. I already spoke with Beth. She told me the whole story." Okay, maybe not the whole story as he hadn't given her a chance, but she'd told him enough. "What were you thinking?"

"Beth did stop by Tangled Charms, but I didn't tell her to sell the house. I would never do such a thing." Jillian sent him a tentative smile. "Sit down and I'll get us some coffee." She stepped into the kitchen area and retrieved two mugs from the cabinet.

He couldn't sit down. He was too worked up. There was something he was missing. But what?

And then he recalled his sister's words. "Beth seems to think if I buy the Crooked S that we'll get together."

Jillian's hand trembled, spilling coffee over the side of the mug. She muttered under her breath as she cleaned up the mess. "I don't know where she would have gotten that idea."

His phone buzzed but he ignored it. "Are you sure?"

Any signs of a smile faded from her face as her eyes narrowed in on him. "Avery Wainwright, I don't know what sort of women you usually run around with, but I have no designs on you. None whatsoever."

"So you're saying you weren't hoping if the family home was sold that you and I…that we'd move into the Crooked S together—"

"No. I didn't. And I wouldn't." She crossed her arms and if looks could kill, he'd be dead on the spot. "You need to take your cat and go. Now."

Chapter Nineteen

I F ONLY IT was that easy…

But every time Avery moved toward the couch, both cats ran as though knowing they were about to be separated. This time they scooted under the couch. Avery smothered a string of colorful words.

He inwardly groaned. He'd definitely rolled out of bed on the wrong side. He sunk down on the throw rug covering the hardwood floor and leaned back against the couch. Maybe he'd reacted too strongly and jumped to the wrong conclusions. But how would his sister have come up with the idea to sell the house without talking to Jillian?

He choked down his pride. "I'm sorry. Would you mind telling me what happened today when you saw my sister?"

Jillian turned around from where she'd perched on one of the two barstools. "Do you really want to know? Or are you going to jump down my throat again?"

"I won't say a word until you're done."

She hesitated as though she wasn't sure she wanted to talk to him. "Beth stopped by the shop. I was surprised to see her, but she said she didn't have classes and wanted to see you take part in the Bake-Off competition."

"Skip to the part about selling the house."

Jillian glowered at him. "I didn't tell her to do that. I mentioned something about her being happy about you attempting to purchase the ranch and she agreed."

"I never mentioned the will to her."

Jillian got a puzzled look on her face. "I'm sorry if I let the cat out of the bag, so to speak. But I didn't know it was a secret."

"So now my sister feels guilty or something and is willing to sacrifice her home to make me happy."

Jillian paused as though giving his statement some thought. "I think it's more than that."

"What's that supposed to mean?"

"I think she's trying to help you."

"I don't need her help."

Jillian arched a brow. "Apparently, aside from baking, you don't need anyone's help. Ever."

"That's about right."

She alighted from the barstool and came over to perch on the edge of the recliner. Her gaze searched him. "Avery, that's no way to live. You have to let people in."

He shook his head. "Things are just fine as is."

"You do realize that your brother is gone. Sure, he'll come back for the occasional holiday, but his life is now in another part of the world. And your sister, she has plans that extend beyond the borders of Marietta."

"This is their home. I'm fixing it up for Beth."

"And so you're going to sacrifice your dreams in order to keep a house that no one wants?"

He shrugged. "I don't know. It just seems so wrong to sell it."

Avery didn't like the way her words poked around the very painful part of his life. It was something he'd never shared with anyone. And he didn't see how revealing his tragic secret would help anything now.

"Avery, talk to me. What aren't you saying?"

It was as though she was reading his mind. He didn't like it. He didn't need her analyzing him and his actions. "Nothing." When she sent him a disbelieving look, he added, "It doesn't matter because it won't change things."

"It might, if you'd talk about it."

"Why do you keep pushing this? It won't undo the damage I've done." And then he realized that in the heat of the moment he'd admitted too much.

Jillian leaned forward, resting her elbows on her knees. "What have you done?"

He sighed as he raked his fingers through his hair. She was never going to give up now. And he didn't need her taking any suspicions to his sister.

What if he just told her? It would satisfy her curiosity. And she would have to agree that he was doing the right thing under the circumstances.

Jillian got up and moved to the couch. She sat close by but she didn't touch him. "Talk to me. You know you can tell me anything."

Normally he'd agree with her, but this was a festering wound that he'd struggled to hide from the rest of the world. Yet with each word that Jillian said, the scabs were being ripped off and the ugly truth was about to escape.

He swallowed hard as he stared straight ahead at the fire crackling in the fireplace. "Way back before my parents died, I knew I hadn't lived up to their expectations. They wanted me to be the first person in the family to go to college, but I just wasn't into learning. Everything I needed to know was at the Crooked S. My mother pleaded with me to do something more constructive with my life, which drove a wedge between us."

Jillian placed a reassuring hand on his arm. "I'm sorry. I didn't know."

"You were the babysitter. How were you supposed to know?"

She withdrew her hand, leaving a cold spot. An awkward silence ensued.

When Avery glanced her way, he found her face pale and her eyes downcast. This really wasn't his day. Now he'd gone and upset the two most important women in his life.

He swallowed hard.

"I didn't mean that the way it sounded. You were more than a babysitter." He struggled to find the right words. "I just meant that my parents tended to keep their opinions private. So they most likely didn't mention anything in front of you."

Her posture seemed to relax a bit. "But I'm certain that they loved you very much. That was abundantly obvious."

"Maybe to you." He moved his arm and his hand brushed over fur. He looked down to find Marshmallow next to him. She glanced up and blinked her blue eyes. He ran his hand over her silky soft fur.

Jillian turned his way. "Did you and your parents have an argument just before the accident?"

He shook his head. "It was quite the opposite." His thoughts went back in time to the point when everything went wrong. "We were actually getting along. I was the points leader in my division and I'd talked them into driving to Wyoming to watch my next competition."

"I remember because they didn't go on overnight trips often and they asked me to stay with the kids."

"In fact, that was the first time they'd ever attended one of my rodeo competitions." The breath hitched in his throat as he recalled what his need of their approval had cost everyone. He continued to pet Marshmallow, who was now lying snug against his thigh. "If…if I hadn't talked them into going, the accident…it wouldn't have happened."

He didn't look at Jillian. There would be sympathy reflected in her eyes. And he didn't deserve anyone's sympathy. Everything that had happened to his family had been his fault. It was his burden to carry for the rest of his life.

"How can you say that?" Jillian moved to the couch. "You weren't the one running from the cops. You didn't T-bone their car."

The memory of his parents' deaths had the back of his eyes burning. He blinked repeatedly. If only…

Jillian's hand rested against his shoulder. He took great comfort in the simple gesture of support. With his free hand, he reached up and covered her hand with his own. He squeezed her hand, drawing on her strength as he finished what he needed to say.

"If I hadn't talked them into that trip, they would still be here for Beth and Jordan. I robbed my brother and sister of their parents. So I can't sell the house—their house. I don't deserve any part of it."

Jillian's hand grasped his shoulder in a firm grip. "You're the only one who believes that. And what about you? You lost the most."

"How do you get that?"

"Because you not only lost your parents, but you sacrificed your youth and dreams in order to be a loving and caring guardian to your siblings as well."

"I did what I had to do, and I'd do it again."

"But what about the future? Your brother and sister are getting on with their lives. You did a great job raising them to be upstanding, independent adults. Now don't you owe it to them to show them that even when life throws you a curve ball you need to make the best of things and move forward?"

"I am making the best of things."

"Are you?" Jillian moved to the floor next to him. "If you remain stuck in the past, you never move forward. They will continually worry about you. They may even give up their dreams to move back here to be with you."

His first reaction was to vehemently disagree with her. After all, what did she know about the situation? And then he realized if anyone knew his family, it was Jillian. She knew every single one of them, including his parents.

Still, this was the first time that she'd ever spoken to him so boldly about something so personal. He looked deep into her eyes. Instead of pity or sympathy, he found compassion and something more. But she glanced away before he could analyze the emotion reflected in her eyes.

He moved his hand as though to reach out to her, to draw her closer. He needed to feel her warm, comforting touch. As she leaned forward, her long golden locks hung down around her face. Once again, he was tempted to feel the silky strands between his fingers.

He reached out, catching a lock with his finger. Instead of glancing away, she continued to hold his stare. There was warmth and understanding in her eyes. Inch by golden inch, he wrapped her hair around his finger. Slowly he drew her closer.

Her gaze never left his. In place of the uncertainty there was now inquisitiveness and—dare he think it—desire. Or was he reflecting his own feelings upon her?

But still, she followed his lead as they drew closer and closer. And then she was there a fraction of an inch away. There was no going back now. His entire being was consumed with his need to feel her lips beneath his.

And then his lips were touching hers. He was gentle—afraid of scaring her away. A tsunami of emotions washed over him, knocking him off balance. It was so unexpected—so moving—that he reached out to her. He gripped her side with one hand and wrapped the other around the back of her neck, holding her close.

This was only supposed to be a simple kiss—nothing more. And yet it was like a chasm had opened up and now he was falling. He'd never ever experienced anything so moving—so gripping.

He pulled back. This wasn't right. Since when did a mere kiss become so intense? It was like he could lose himself in the kiss, but he didn't do that—he didn't lose control.

Jillian blinked and pulled back. She didn't say anything, but she was studying him. He stared straight ahead at the window, but he could feel her ever-present gaze on him.

He didn't know what to say. He didn't know exactly what had happened just now. And so he opted to ignore it and pretend that it had never happened.

Jillian leaned back. "Where does this kiss leave us?"

The breath caught in his throat. He was in trouble. He didn't want to encourage this talk. He didn't have the answers she wanted. He didn't even know what the answers were.

"Aren't you even going to look at me?" she asked.

He didn't want to. He knew he wasn't going to like what he found. He'd screwed up. Again. He shouldn't have kissed her. Jillian was different from other women. She wasn't one to take relationships lightly. When she babysat for his brother and sister, she took it seriously and really cared about them. So much so that she still kept in contact with both of his siblings.

By now, he thought he'd have something substantial to offer her. But none of his attempts to buy the ranch had panned out. And Jillian deserves so much more than this rodeo cowboy could offer her.

"There's something I need to tell you. I'm leaving town."

"To go back to the rodeo?"

He nodded. "It's my last chance to gain the money I need to buy the Crooked S. I've tried everything else and nothing has worked out."

"And when did you decide this?"

"Today."

He turned his head and his gaze met hers. In the depths of her blue eyes, he found confusion and anger. He knew Jillian wanted a calm stable life, but he wasn't in a position to offer that to her. Everything about his life was up in the air. "That kiss shouldn't have happened. It was a mistake."

Her gaze narrowed. "Well, that makes it all the better."

"What's that supposed to mean? If you're worried about Glenn—"

"I'm not." And then ever so softly under her breath, Jillian uttered, "She was right."

"Who was? Right about what?"

"My mother." Jillian shook her head. "Never mind. It doesn't matter."

He had a feeling he'd missed something important, but she'd turned away. He reached out as though to gain her attention but hesitated. The last thing in the world he wanted to do was hurt her. But at this point he still had nothing to offer her. His hand lowered to his side where it brushed against Romeo, who'd settled between Avery and Jillian.

He'd never really given much thought to cats. He was a horse man. But he was starting to understand what was so special about cats. They were independent, full of personality, and caring.

He moved his hand slowly, not sure if Romeo would allow Avery to pet him. To Avery's surprise, not only did the cat allow him, but Romeo started to purr too. He'd at least won over someone this evening.

When Jillian's gaze finally met his, she said, "You do have another choice. You could take your sister and brother up on their offer. At least hear them out. You don't necessarily have to agree with their plan of action, but you need to respect the fact that they love you enough to do this for you."

She never ceased to amaze him. Even after what they'd just been through, she was still trying to help him. She would make some man an amazing wife.

"I just don't know if I can do what they want. I don't feel like I deserve such a big sacrifice."

"You do deserve it." She lifted her hand and cupped his cheek. "You are the only one who ever thought the accident had anything to do with you. Everyone else blamed the criminal who was evading the police. They all considered it a horrific accident. Lighten up on yourself."

Avery's phone buzzed. He answered it. It was Beth, worried about Marshmallow. He promised to bring the cat right home.

At the doorway, Avery paused. His gaze met Jillian's once more. With the cat in his arms, he couldn't do what he wanted to do—pull Jillian close and kiss her again. It was for the best.

Instead, he had to settle for words. "Thank you. For everything."

"You'll hear your sister out before you decide anything?"

He nodded. "I will."

Avery walked away, surprised by the events of the evening. He'd come here certain he knew what was best for everyone. And now he was walking away with Jillian's words buzzing around in his mind. Was she right? Should he let his brother and sister make this sacrifice? And if he were to accept his family's help, was it too much to think this just might be the necessary step to finally win over Jillian?

Chapter Twenty

I CAN DO THIS.
    I. Can. Do. This.

Avery's whole body was tense as he entered the Main Street Diner for round two of the Bake-Off. The power of positive thinking was failing him today. He wasn't worried so much about himself, but rather about Jillian. By now, everyone in Marietta knew that she was mentoring him, and he didn't want to let her down.

He'd arrived early, hoping to get familiar with his surroundings and settle his nerves. But now that he was here, he was more nervous than ever.

Before checking out his work space, he needed to do something important. He wanted to make a sizable donation to Harry's House and he knew exactly how to do it. He glanced around, finding that Jillian had her wristbands as well as her wire necklace and earrings on display. She'd worked so hard on them and it showed. They were stunning and they'd look amazing on Jillian.

His gaze strayed across the room to where Jillian was

speaking with the judges. Her back was to him and so he made his way over to where the bid sheets were and grabbed one. As quickly as he could, he wrote out an amount he was certain no one would outbid. And then he dropped it in the jar.

Feeling as though he'd just gotten away with it, he turned around and bumped into Jillian's mother. She frowned at him. He'd always had the feeling she didn't like him, but he didn't understand why.

"Hello, Mrs. Parker." He forced a smile to his lips.

She didn't smile back. "I see your house is up for sale."

"It is." Though he still had his reservations, he'd given in to his siblings' plan.

Mrs. Parker nodded. "You've been seeing a lot of my daughter lately."

"She's been a huge help getting me ready for the competition."

The woman studied him for a moment. The intensity of her stare made him want to turn away, but he stood his ground. If he ever wanted to win over the daughter, he'd need to win over the mother.

"What exactly is going on between you and my daughter?"

He swallowed hard. "We're friends."

"But you want it to be more than that?"

Wow. She wasn't going to lighten up on him. He supposed he deserved it. "I, uh, like your daughter."

"Listen, if you are just going to string her along and hurt her again, back away now."

"But we aren't dating. She's seeing someone else."

Her mother's eyes widened. "She is? This is news to me." Mrs. Parker's gaze sought out her daughter. "Perhaps I'll go have a word with her."

Avery found it strange that Jillian wouldn't tell her mother about Glenn, but maybe she was worried her mother wouldn't like him. And for good reason too. Glenn wasn't exactly the friendliest sort of guy—at least not the side of Glenn that Avery had seen.

He didn't have long to think over his conversation with Jillian's mother. He had more pressing matters on his mind. Right about now, Avery was regretting going along with this Bake-Off competition. Even though he'd baked three pies, he'd only produced one that made Jillian smile when it came out of the oven.

This event was making him way more nervous than the first round of baking. He didn't even want to contemplate what it would be like to make a cake. The pie seemed challenging enough. He hoped he wouldn't do anything to embarrass Jillian. He just needed to get through the pie portion of the contest without burning anything this time.

Avery headed to his station and put on his apron as Mrs. Monroe made the kickoff speech. As soon as the announcement concluded, Avery began putting together the ingredients for the pie crust.

His hands had a slight tremble as he cut the butter into the flour mixture. He struggled to get the dough to come together properly; then he recalled what Jillian had taught him about adding additional water to get the mixture to the right consistency. And it worked.

By the time he had the rolling pin out, he was starting to feel a bit more confident. He got all of the ingredients for the filling out. He just had to add everything at the appropriate time.

He glanced up every so often to check on Jillian. He didn't know why, he just liked knowing she was close by. And that's when he noticed she was speaking to someone. When the man glanced up, Avery recognized him—Glenn. And he didn't look happy. Avery couldn't help but wonder what was going on with them.

It was none of his business so he turned his attention to the bowl where he was measuring out the ingredients for the pie filling. He added sugar, cinnamon, salt—his gaze strayed back to Jillian.

Jerky arm movements said that the conversation had deteriorated. And now Jillian was frowning and pointing to the door, but Glenn was shaking his head.

Avery wasn't going to stand for Glenn bullying Jillian. He set down the measuring cup, not the least bit worried about the pie at this point. He ignored the judges' comments as he moved away from his station. He'd be back just as soon as he made sure everything was all right with Jillian.

"What's going on here?" Avery asked, bringing the heated conversation between Jillian and Glen to a halt.

"I've got this," Jillian said.

Glenn crossed his arms and glared at Avery. "Yeah, butt out. This is private."

Avery's gaze moved between the two of them. Was this a lover's quarrel or something more?

"Glenn was just leaving." Jillian glared at Glenn.

The man turned on Avery. "This is your fault. Everything would have been fine if you hadn't come back to town."

Avery refused to react to Glenn's barbed comment. "The lady asked you to leave and I'd suggest you do it. Unless you need help out."

Glenn hesitated before turning to Jillian.

"Just go," she said. "We'll talk later."

Glenn strode away.

Talk later? Avery was disappointed to hear that Jillian wasn't going to kick the man to the curb straightaway. What did she see in this man? It was totally beyond Avery's comprehension.

"What are you still dealing with him for?" Avery blurted out in frustration.

Jillian shook her head. "You don't understand. And I'm not getting into it here."

"But he doesn't even make you happy—"

"Avery, stop. I'm not discussing Glenn with you. It's my

problem. I'll fix it."

He understood enough to know that she hadn't washed her hands of that jerk.

"What are you doing over here? You're supposed to be baking."

And then he remembered how he'd walked off halfway through making the pie filling. As he rushed back to his station, he realized one thing. He cared far too much about Jillian to stick around and watch her waste her life with that loser. The rodeo circuit was starting to look very appealing.

Lost in his conflicted thoughts, Avery picked up the measuring spoon he had left on the counter and added the salt followed by the remaining ingredients. Then he added the filling to the pie crust and proceeded to assemble the pie top just like he'd practiced.

At last, he slipped the pie in the oven.

Avery felt confident this time. He was happy to redeem himself for the Monroes' sake. The pie was picture-perfect. Some of his finest work.

While the pies baked, it was time to announce the winner's name for Jillian's jewelry auction. Avery had forgotten about his bid until that point. He wished he hadn't come up with the idea, but now it was too late. So he leaned back and watched the proceedings.

After Jillian said a few words, she reached out as Suzanna placed the highest bidder's information into her hand. "And the winner is," she unfolded the paper and paused, "um, it's

Avery Wainwright."

A murmur rippled through the crowd and then the clapping began. He had won the necklace and earrings. Avery made his way to the front of the crowd. He'd never seen Jillian's face so red.

When he approached her, she leaned over and whispered, "You shouldn't have done this. But thank you. I hope Beth enjoys the set."

"But they aren't for Beth." When her eyes filled with questions, he said, "They are for you. They're almost as beautiful as you."

"But I...um, I don't know what to say."

"Just turn around and let me put it on you."

She shook her head. "I can't wear them. It wouldn't be right."

Her refusal to wear the jewelry deflated his happiness. It was just one more reminder of the tension lingering between them. His gut twisted in a knot.

When she turned away to speak to another person, Avery placed the black velvet box holding the beautiful jewelry next to her purse. He just hoped she would keep the jewelry. After all, she deserved to wear her own creation.

THE PIES WERE done at last.

The eight contestants lined up behind their entries.

Avery was nervous. He held his hands behind his back to keep from fidgeting. His pie looked amazing, especially considering last week he didn't have a clue how to bake one.

Though the crust hadn't browned evenly, the lattice was evenly distributed and the caramel sauce had really added an extra oomph. When the judges made it to him, he straightened his shoulders and waited. First they judged the pie's appearance and a few other criteria.

And then it was time for the most important element—the taste test.

The breath caught in Avery's throat as each judge slipped a fork into their piece of pie. And then one by one they lifted their forks and took a bite. And just as quickly each judge frowned.

"Ugh." Ryan Henderson, a top pastry chef, frowned as he set his fork on the plate. His gaze met Avery's. "I think you got too much salt in it."

The other three judges nodded in agreement.

In that moment, Avery realized what he'd done wrong. He'd let himself become distracted with Jillian. In the process, he'd added salt not once but twice. How could he have let himself become distracted again?

As his spirits deflated, the air in his lungs escaped.

Today just wasn't his day.

Chapter Twenty-One

WITH A YANK, the For Sale sign was once more removed.

Monday morning, Avery trudged up to the garbage can and placed it there, for the final time. At least, the realtor had been too busy to put in one of those big wooden signs. This was just a little sign with metal prongs.

Upon entering the house, he realized he should call the realtor and take the house off the market. He didn't know what he was thinking agreeing to sell his childhood home—his brother and sister's last link to their parents. The memories in the house were more important than owning a ranch. At least that's what he kept telling himself.

Rick Styles, owner of Styles Realty, answered on the second ring. Before Avery could get to the point of the phone call, Rick wanted to talk about the Bake-Off. Avery didn't want to be rude and settled for making small talk until it seemed like an appropriate point to segue the conversation to taking the house off the market.

"Are you sure this is what you want to do?" Rick asked,

taking some liberties since he'd known Avery all of his life. "When I last spoke with you and your sister, you both seemed so certain it was the right thing to do."

Beth didn't know about Avery changing his mind. She was now back at school and he wasn't ready to tell her about his decision. She'd launch into another of her long-winded speeches about how he was making all of the wrong choices with his life. Since when had their roles reversed where she was advising him on his life choices?

Avery sat down on the living room couch and stared at the mess of paperwork awaiting him. "I'll take care of Beth."

"But I don't understand," Rick said, "your sister seemed certain about this last week. I'm not concerned about the loss on the sale. I just want to make sure you're making the best decision for you and your family."

"A lot can change in a weekend." Avery's thoughts strayed back to the Bake-Off. He'd desperately wanted Jillian to end things once and for all with Glenn, but she hadn't. And though their relationship appeared stormy, she still cared enough about the man to try and talk things out. Frustration balled up in Avery's gut.

If she couldn't see what a loser Glenn was, there was nothing Avery could do. She'd made her choice and now it was time for him to put as much distance between them as possible.

Maybe with time and space, he'd get her out of his system. Something told him that was more wishful thinking than anything else. Jillian was in his mind, his blood, and most of all his heart.

What did it hurt to tell Rick about his decision? Soon everyone would know. Avery leaned back on the couch. "I've decided not to settle down. I'll be heading back out on the rodeo circuit right after the last round of the Bake-Off. So I won't have time to run a ranch."

"I see." Rick sounded disappointed, but he didn't push the matter any further. "It'll take a day or two to pull the listing from the various real estate websites."

"I understand. And thank you. I'm sorry for putting you through all of the trouble."

"It happens. Just let me know if you ever decide to put the house back on the market. You've done an amazing job with the place and I think when the time is right, it'll sell quickly."

Avery appreciated Rick's kind words about his remodel job. He thanked him for everything and promised that if he needed a realtor he would be the first person he called.

He was still holding the phone in his hand when it rang. "Hello."

"Can we talk?" Jillian asked.

"I don't think that's a good idea." He didn't want to get involved in whatever was going on with her and Glenn. And if he saw her right now, he would tell her exactly what he had on his mind. It wouldn't do either of them any good. "Besides, I'm headed out to check on my horse."

"This won't take long. I'm right outside."

She was? He moved to the living room and glanced out the window. Her car was parked along the curb. "How long have you been sitting there?"

"I just pulled up. I kept trying to call, but your line was busy and I wanted to take care of this before work."

"Jillian, I don't think this is a good idea—"

"It won't take long at all. I promise."

It went against his better judgment but he said, "Come in."

He propped the door open and waited for her to make her way up the walk. When she stepped up on the porch, he moved aside to allow her entrance to the house.

He closed the door and turned to her. "What can I do for you?"

"I noticed the For Sale sign is missing from the yard. Did the house sell?"

He shook his head. "I took it off the market."

"Oh." Her expressive blue eyes reflected the passage of varying thoughts that had crossed her mind. "I stopped by to let you know I don't think we're working well together. I'm sorry you didn't win either of the first two rounds of the competition."

"It's not you. It's me."

She held up her hand, halting his explanation. "This arrangement isn't working for either of us. But I have lined up someone to help you with the last round of the competition."

He knew Jillian backing out of mentoring him had nothing to do with his performance at the Bake-Off and more to do with them. She was outright rejecting him, fully and completely. Avery refused to acknowledge the stab of pain that thought brought him.

He mentally chastised himself for following his heart instead of his brain and avoiding any messy emotional entanglements. Why had he gone there with Jillian? He'd opened himself up as much as he could but it wasn't enough for her.

He drew his thoughts up short. Her reasons didn't matter. He was fooling himself to think they would ever have worked as a couple.

"Who is this person who's supposed to help me?" he asked, hoping it wasn't her mother.

"It's Suzanna. She's even better than me in the kitchen. So she'll be a big help to you with the cake. She'll stop over tomorrow at six-thirty."

Crash!

The sound of shattering glass echoed through the house. Avery turned toward the bedrooms. "I better check on that. I'll be back."

WITH AVERY OUT of the room, Jillian drew her first easy

breath.

She didn't know how difficult this visit was going to be. She hadn't even known if she was doing the right thing. But she felt awful that Avery hadn't done very well at the Bake-Off and she blamed herself. Even if he wouldn't admit it, he blamed her too. His temperament changed every time he was around her.

Resolute to clear the air between them, Jillian moved to the couch. As she sat down, she noticed the array of papers covering the coffee table. She shouldn't look. It was none of her business, but as she went to turn away, her gaze strayed over the word rodeo.

At this point, she just couldn't resist looking at the papers. There were rodeo schedules, entry forms, and instructions on closing a house for an extended period. With each word she read, her heart sunk.

The worst thing had happened—she'd fallen in love with Avery again and he was leaving town. The backs of her eyes stung, causing her to blink repeatedly. From the looks of it, he would be gone for a very long time. She knew the rodeo was in his blood. Why did she think that would ever change?

She got to her feet and headed for the door. And then reaching in her purse for the car keys, her hand strayed across the velvet jewelry box containing the jewelry he'd won at the Bake-Off that weekend.

She couldn't keep it. Every time she looked at the necklace, she would be reminded of Avery. It would be too painful of a memory.

She slipped the box from her purse and retraced her steps to the coffee table. She set it down in the middle of the papers before letting herself quietly out the front door. There was nothing left for them to say to each other.

Chapter Twenty-Two

H E WASN'T CHANGING his mind.

Avery paced back and forth in the kitchen. He'd just hung up the phone after speaking once more with Rick at the real estate office. There was an offer for the house. It had been made before Rick could pull the listing.

When Rick had tried to explain to the buyers that the house was no longer available, they wouldn't take no for an answer. They'd been one of the first people to tour it in the few days that it was on the market and they'd fallen in love with it. And now they were offering above asking price to purchase it.

Before he'd hung up, Rick had told Avery to sleep on it. And Avery had agreed. Money from the sale plus the money he'd squirreled away this year would be enough to secure a loan to buy Crooked S Ranch. Not that he was really going to do it. This town was too small for him to avoid Jillian and right now, it would be too painful to stick around, especially if she worked things out with Glenn. The thought twisted his gut up in a knot.

The doorbell rang. It would be Suzanna. He glanced up at the clock. Six-thirty, right on the dot. She was nothing if not punctual.

He didn't know Suzanna very well. They shared the occasional hello but not much more. And now as they worked to separate egg whites into a large mixing bowl, he found he liked her. She was friendly, considerate, and smart. No wonder she was Jillian's best friend.

As he followed her directions and whisked the egg whites to soft peaks, she asked him, "Have you known Blake long?"

"I've known him since he started working at the Crooked S Ranch about nine or so years ago. He's a really good guy."

"That's what I thought too."

He had the feeling after spotting Suzanna and Blake in deep conversation at the Bake-Off that there was a romance budding. "Is there anything else you'd like to know?"

"Can you keep a secret?"

"I can." He had a feeling he knew what she was about to tell him.

Even though it was just the two of them in the house, she whispered, "Blake asked me out, but I haven't told anyone."

Avery wasn't sure how to react so he settled for, "I hope you have a good time."

It took him a while to get used to folding in the flour. As Suzanna explained the reason for folding the flour in versus whisking it, he worried that he would stir the batter too much and the cake would go flat. He was not enjoying this tedious and stressful part of the process. Knowing his luck, he'd end up with a pancake.

At this point, he had no illusion about winning the Bake-Off. None whatsoever. But he'd pledged to do his best so that's what he'd do. And afterward, he'd pack up and leave town. The further away he went, the better.

But there was one thing that was still bothering him. Try as he might, he just didn't get the whole Glenn and Jillian thing. At first, he thought she might be dazzled because Glenn was flashy with nice clothes and a fancy car, but surely she'd seen past all of that by now. Maybe he needed another perspective.

After sliding the angel food cake in the oven and setting the timer, Avery turned to Suzanna. "What does Jillian see in Glenn?"

Suzanna's eyes widened. "I…I don't think I'm the person to ask."

"I just don't get it. Sure he might have some money and maybe women think he's good-looking, but he doesn't seem very nice."

Suzanna crossed her arms and leaned back against the counter. "I didn't know you knew Glenn that well."

"I don't. But we've had a couple of run-ins. I just keep thinking Jillian can do better."

Suzanna smiled. "You're jealous."

"I am not." *Liar. Liar.*

Suzanna arched a brow. "You are. It's written all over your face."

"It doesn't matter if I am. Jillian made it clear she still has unfinished business with that man. I don't know why I ever thought there could be something between us."

"Oh boy, you have it bad for her."

He shook his head. "It doesn't matter now. I'm leaving town."

"Heading back to the rodeo?"

"It's where I belong."

"Would you say the same thing if I told you there is absolutely nothing romantic going on between Jillian and Glenn?"

"But this weekend at the Bake-Off, I heard them. It isn't over."

Suzanna paused as though considering her options. "I'm going to tell you something that could get us both in trouble with Jillian, but I think you deserve to know."

His curiosity was piqued now. "What is it?"

"The only thing between Jillian and Glenn is that he tried to use her and Tangled Charms to secure a loan. Apparently he's in deep financial trouble."

"Really?" Avery never would have guessed any of this. "And Jillian didn't know about it?"

"Not until the bank called her."

"But why didn't she say anything to me?"

"My guess is her pride got in the way. She was embarrassed she ever dated him and she was trying to get him out of her life as quietly as possible—but Glenn isn't good at taking a hint or even a blunt statement."

"Are you sure?"

"I'm sure she's been in love with you since she was a teenager. She tried to move on, but once you came back in her life for the Bake-Off, she couldn't deny her feelings."

It was Avery's turn to lean back against the opposite counter as he digested this news. What did this all mean? Had he totally misread everything?

Suzanna moved to start cleaning the kitchen island. "I think you're foolish if you let Jillian get away again." Her pointed words sliced into his thoughts. Suzanna continued. "Most people only get one shot at love. You've now had two chances with Jillian. You won't get another one. So don't waste this opportunity."

Her profound words struck him. The truth was he loved Jillian more than he thought possible. And he knew it was one of those once-in-a-lifetime loves. That's why he was planning to leave Marietta. He just couldn't bear to be so close to her and yet so far away.

But now—now he knew what he had to do.

He just had to hope it wasn't too late.

Chapter Twenty-Three

THIS COULD BE the biggest mistake of his life…

Or it could be his smartest move.

Avery dismissed the contradictory thoughts. They were of no help and they were starting to give him a headache.

It all boiled down to the fact that he had to do something drastic because there was no way he could lose Jillian. He knew an apology for not being the man she needed him to be in the past wouldn't be enough. He had to show her that he'd changed. And he was willing to risk everything to make things right with her.

He chose to walk to the Graff Hotel for the final round of the Bake-Off. The physical exertion of walking in the chilly February air was just what he needed to clear his head. Between the competition and trying to win over Jillian, he was a bundle of nerves.

Tonight not only would he be putting his limited baking skills on display for the town, but he also planned to make his feelings for Jillian known to everyone. That was not an easy feat for a cowboy who was used to keeping everything inside.

When his parents died, he'd learned to keep his emotions tucked inside where no one could see them. After all, he'd suddenly gone from the cool big brother to a fill-in parent who had no clue what he was doing. And his siblings had needed all of the support and security that he could muster.

He never knew by stifling his emotions that he'd also miss what was right in front of him—the best thing in his life—Jillian. He just hoped it wasn't too late to convince her to give him another chance to get this right.

The closer he got to the hotel, the faster he moved. He pulled out his phone and texted Suzanna to make sure Jillian would be at the event. His finger moved rapidly over the screen.

> **Avery:** How's our plan going?
>
> **Suzanna:** Hit a few snags but everything is now on track. I'll get her there but the rest is up to you.
>
> **Avery:** Understood.
>
> **Suzanna:** How's your end of the plan?

Avery felt around in his pocket until he found the integral part of the evening.

> **Avery:** I've got it all under control.
>
> **Suzanna:** Are you sure about this? Don't hurt her again or you'll have me to answer to.
>
> **Avery:** I won't. I promise.
>
> **Suzanna:** I'm holding you to that promise.

Avery: *See you soon.*

Suzanna: *Good luck!*

He'd take all of the luck that he could get at this point. He just had to be successful this evening. He didn't have a backup plan.

For this round, he had to bake a cake. This should be interesting. Baking a pie was one thing—it's pretty hard to mess up, so long as you sufficiently flour the countertop and only add the salt once. He inwardly groaned, remembering his ridiculous mistake.

But baking a cake from scratch was even more complicated. And what had he been thinking when he picked out an angel food cake? Surely there had to be easier cakes, right?

He was doomed to fail. He was certain of it. He had no illusions about winning this round. He would just be happy to have a cake that wasn't a gooey glob of a mess. If it was at all possible, he wanted to be able to hold his head up in public when this was all said and done.

Now within sight of the hotel, he noticed the bumper-to-bumper parking. The whole town was really pulling together and coming out in support. Which just made it all the more stressful for him. Thankfully all of his supplies were already at the hotel or else he was certain that he would have forgotten at least two or three ingredients.

He was never this nervous for his appearances on the rodeo circuit. Probably because when he was astride a bucking bronc, he felt in control. He'd spent most of his life around animals and understood them better than he understood most humans.

But this baking stuff was a real challenge for him—if it wasn't for Jillian, he would have never made it this far. No matter how bad things had gotten, she'd been there for him. Even arranging for Suzanna to coach him through this last part.

Now, the time had come for the third and final round. It just didn't feel right not having Jillian here beside him. He planned to change those circumstances as soon as possible.

He entered the hotel lobby and looked around for Jillian, but she was nowhere to be found. He refused to worry. Suzanna had assured him that Jillian would be there.

In no time, the competition was under way. Avery gave all of his attention to the cake. It had to be perfect. He whisked the egg whites...and whisked them...and whisked them. He'd learned the hard way that if he didn't beat them enough the cake would not be light and fluffy. And if he overbeat them, the egg whites would separate. It was a fine line to get it right.

Kind of like his relationship with Jillian. If he didn't say enough, she'd be gone for good. And if he said too much, she'd be gone too. So he'd been practicing what he'd say for the past two days.

A hush had fallen over the audience as they watched each bachelor create their cake. Mrs. Monroe did a great job as the announcer. She even did the soft voice like a golf announcer on television. She told everyone what the bachelors were baking and a little background information about each entrant.

By the time his cake was baked, Avery was a nervous wreck. His big moment was almost here. He had it all worked out in his head.

As the judges made their way down the line sampling everyone's cake, he pulled out the special cupcake that he'd baked for Jillian with a diamond centerpiece.

He hoped Jillian would be impressed. He glanced around for her. She was nowhere to be found. His blood pressure rose. Where could she be?

And then he spotted Suzanna. She shook her head.

His heart sank.

All of his planning had failed.

Chapter Twenty-Four

SHOULD SHE HAVE gone to the Bake-Off?

Jillian paced back and forth in her apartment. No, she was fine right here. She didn't have a vested interest in the final round.

To her surprise, her mother was not happy that Jillian had backed out of going to the Bake-Off. Her mother insisted that if she was staying home she could at least keep Romeo company. Jillian didn't want company. She longed for the solitude. Yet, it was easier to do as her mother asked than to argue the point.

When her mother inquired about her reason for staying home, Jillian had claimed a headache. It wasn't exactly a lie. Her head was abuzz with thoughts of Avery. Suzanna had given her a heads-up that he'd planned something special for this evening and he wanted her there. Jillian had no idea what he had planned and Suzanna hadn't given her any details.

So what was Avery up to?

And what did it have to do with her?

Then a sobering thought hit her. Perhaps he was going to announce at the Bake-Off that he was leaving town. It would be his swan song of sorts where he told the whole town goodbye at once. That must be it.

Still, she felt bad for letting Suzanna down. They'd planned to go to the Bake-Off together. She glanced at the clock. Perhaps it wasn't too late to go. Saying goodbye to Avery might be the closure she needed—a chance to close this chapter in her life once and for all.

Before she could change her mind, she grabbed her coat. She moved to the door and pulled it open. In that moment, Romeo dashed out the door.

"Romeo! Come back!"

Romeo had been so well behaved lately that she thought he'd gotten past his fascination with the great outdoors. She had obviously been wrong. And so started another round of chasing Romeo through the streets of Marietta.

HE HADN'T WON the Bake-Off.

His plan to win over Jillian had failed.

And yet Avery refused to give up. The truth was he hadn't failed with Jillian because he hadn't found her yet to put his plan into action.

And that's why he was out driving around Marietta after the Bake-Off ended.

He'd checked Tangled Charms and then her apartment. He'd banged on her door but she hadn't answered. He didn't know where else she could be. He had no choice but to head home—alone.

He glanced at the two jewelry boxes on the seat next to him in the pickup. He didn't know what he was going to do with them. Maybe some sleep would help him focus and regroup.

He backed out of Jillian's driveway. Surely she hadn't left town. Was she really that upset with him?

He decided to try calling her again. He'd just turned on-to his street. Before he could reach for his phone, he spotted her car parked along the curb. Jillian was here?

His spirits buoyed, he wheeled into his driveway and threw the pickup into Park. There could only be one reason she was here—she still cared. His heart swelled in his chest.

He grabbed the jewelry boxes from the seat. He jumped out of the truck and placed the ring box in his jacket pocket. During the time he'd been searching for her, he'd been thinking that he needed more of a lead-up to the big moment. He had to make sure she understood just how much he loved her.

He made his way along the walk to the front porch where he found Jillian sitting on the steps. "Hi."

She glanced up at him. "Hi. I bet you didn't expect to see me tonight."

"Actually, I've been looking for you." And then realizing

she must be freezing out here, he said, "Why don't we go inside?"

Jillian hesitated.

"Is there something wrong?"

She sighed. "It's Romeo. He escaped again and I was hoping he would come here."

"It's all the more reason for you to come inside. I'm sure he'll show up soon."

Jillian got to her feet and looked around the darkened yard before her gaze came back to rest on Avery. "Are you sure you don't mind?"

"Not at all. There's something I needed to discuss with you."

Once their coats were off, Jillian took a seat in the armchair next to the couch. Avery perched on the end of the couch closest to her. His heart was racing as he realized he only had one chance to get his proposal right.

He cleared his throat. "First of all, these are yours." He held out the large velvet box containing the necklace and earrings she'd made. "I bid on these for you and I really want you to have them."

There was uncertainty reflected in her eyes, but she accepted the jewelry case. Looking uncomfortable, she said, "I heard you're leaving town tomorrow. I should go so you can pack or make whatever arrangements you need to."

"I've changed my mind. I'm staying." He could see his announcement surprised her. "And you should know that

I've sold the house."

Her eyes widened. "You bought the ranch?"

He nodded, hoping it would please her.

"That's wonderful." She smiled. And suddenly the tension between them seemed to ease. "I'm so happy for you."

"The thing is, it's a big ranch and it can get awfully lonely." He watched as an array of emotions were reflected in her eyes. "How do you feel about ranches?"

"Me?" She pressed a hand to her chest.

"Jillian, I've handled this situation poorly and for that I'm sorry. At first, I thought you were still involved with Glenn—"

"I'm not. At least not romantically. I should have made that clearer."

"Suzanna set me straight on a few matters unrelated to cake making when she was here. And I am very grateful to her."

"You are?"

He nodded. "She encouraged me to follow my heart—to take a chance on the future and make my dreams come true."

Jillian looked disappointed. "Oh, you mean the ranch."

"No, I mean you." His heart was pounding so hard that it echoed in his ears. "I love you, Jillian. I can't imagine my life without you in it." And then remembering the ring, he said, "Wait right here."

He rushed over to where he'd placed his coat, and with

shaky hands he removed the ring box from his pocket. She hadn't bolted out the door so he had to hope that was a good sign.

When he returned to her, he dropped down on one knee and held the box out to her. "Jillian, would you do me the honor of becoming my wife?"

A tear dripped onto her cheek. His body tensed. *Please let it be a tear of joy.*

The next thing he knew, Jillian was kneeling on the floor next to him. Her gaze met his. There was clarity reflected in her beautiful blue eyes. "I love you too. But are you sure about this? You want to start over with your own family?"

"I'm positive. I tried to tell myself that I was happy out on the road. Then returning and roaming through this house all alone, I knew I was kidding myself. I want to build a life with you."

"And a couple of babies?"

"Them too."

"What changed your mind?"

Avery understood her need for clarity. It had taken him a long time to get to this point. "I realized this living alone isn't what I want after all. Being a bachelor isn't all it's cracked up to be. So what do you say? Do you want to grow old with me?"

"Yes." She leaned forward, pressing her lips to his.

It all felt so right—so perfect.

A scratching sound interrupted the moment. Soon a meow followed. With a groan, they pulled apart. Avery hesitated to let her go, but he smiled, realizing there would be a lifetime of kisses. They were both smiling when they got to their feet.

When he opened the door, Romeo ran inside. "Hello, fella."

Romeo murred in response, causing Jillian and Avery to laugh.

Just then Marshmallow entered the living room. The cats sniffed each other and then ran off.

"Looks like everyone is happy." Avery smiled at Jillian. And then realizing he still had the ring, he moved to her side. "We forgot this."

And with that he slid the diamond ring on her finger and sealed the deal with a kiss.

Epilogue

Fifteen months later...

I F THIS WAS a dream, he never wanted to wake up.

Avery stood in the living room of the log home that he now shared with Jillian. He turned to the wall of windows that overlooked the Crooked S Ranch. For the first time in his life, he felt truly at home. He stared off into the distance at his ranch—their beautiful ranch.

It was hard to believe that after such a rough patch in his life everything had come together so well. It might not have been an easy transition, but it was so worth it.

And he couldn't have done any of it without Jillian. She had always been there when he needed her. She was his source of strength when he felt weak. She was his best friend. And he tried his best to be those things for her.

"Hey, husband, what are you doing in here? Shouldn't you be out tending to the livestock?"

He turned to find Jillian standing there with a kitten in each arm, one black and white, just like Romeo, while the other kitten was all white. His wife smiled broadly. "Aren't we lucky that your sister decided not to stand in the way of true love?"

"What?"

"You know, letting my mother take Marshmallow so the cats could be together. Now they'll live happily ever after." Jillian held out the squirmy black and white kitten named Oreo. "And they make such cute kittens."

Avery cradled Oreo in his arms, having a hard time keeping ahold of it as the kitten was in a constant state of motion. "Too bad your mother got Marshmallow and Romeo fixed. I could get used to having more kittens around the house. They are really smart."

His wife sent him a puzzled look. "How do you get that?"

"They got us together, didn't they?"

Jillian laughed. "Is that what happened?"

Avery nodded. "Romeo is a natural-born matchmaker."

"Well, you don't have to worry. These two furbabies are ours."

"Are you sure they're old enough to leave their mother?"

Jillian nodded. "Positive. But I had to promise my mother that we'd bring them back to visit."

Avery laughed. "I think we can do that. What about the other kittens?"

"Well, Suzanna is taking one. My mother is keeping one so it's not so hard for Marshmallow. And your sister wants one. Speaking of Beth, she phoned and wants to know if she can bring home her new boyfriend next weekend."

"She's never brought home a guy." Avery wasn't sure what to make of it. "Should I be worried?"

Jillian shrugged. "I don't know, but she sounded really happy on the phone. We could make it a dinner party and invite Blake and Suzanna over too."

"They've been seeing a lot of each other."

"Yes, they have."

Just the way his wife said that clued him in that he was missing something. "What don't I know?"

"Well, it's not for sure, but I think there might be wedding bells in their future."

"And how do you feel about that?" He'd learned that his wife had a good sense of people.

"I think they make each other very happy. They belong together." Jillian moved to the couch with the kitten. "One more thing. There's an email from Jordan. He's been reassigned to Germany."

Avery wasn't happy to have his brother so far from home, but he was happy that Jordan was following his dreams. "I'll email him back this evening."

Jillian placed the little white kitten, named Snowball, on the floor. "Can you watch them both for a second?"

He nodded. "Where are you going?"

"You'll find out."

In the end, he may have lost that long-ago Bake-Off, but he'd won the most important thing in the world—the woman he loved. He had no idea that entering the competition would open his eyes to the important things around him.

The funny thing was he thought by being a rodeo cowboy that he took risks and lived on the edge. It wasn't until taking part in the Bachelor Bake-Off that he realized just how guarded he'd really been.

The greatest challenge in his life had been putting his heart out there on the line. And now that he had Jillian in his life, he knew just how amazing life could be. He regretted wasting so much time figuring it all out.

Jillian returned with two slices of pie and handed one over. "I found some apples in the fridge and thought I'd use them up. But if you don't want any, I can give your slice to someone else—"

"Oh no, this belongs to me." He accepted the plate. He glanced over it. "How come this pie looks so familiar?"

"Because I used the same recipe you used for the Bake-Off."

"I see. And is there any special reason for this treat in the middle of the afternoon?" He sensed that something was up, but he couldn't quite put his finger on what it might be.

His wife glanced away and shrugged, but there was clearly a smile on her face.

"Okay. Out with it."

"How would you feel about some more family living here at the ranch with us?"

"Besides your mother?"

Jillian smiled and nodded.

Construction had already started on her mother's house on the property. Her mother wanted to be close to her daughter, but not crowd them by living under the same roof, so they'd compromised on a small house not far from the main house.

So if Jillian wasn't talking about her mother, was she referring to Jordan or Beth? He'd welcome them anytime. It was a given that the Crooked S was their home for whenever or however long they needed it.

"I don't mind. You know that I love our family."

"Good to know."

"When are they arriving?"

"Oh, I'd say in seven or so months."

His gaze narrowed. "We aren't talking about Jordan or Beth, are we?"

Jillian's smile broadened as she shook her head.

His heart started to pound in his chest. "Are you saying what I think you're saying?"

"Avery, you're going to be a daddy."

"Woohoo!" And then he wrapped his free arm around his wife's waist and pulled her close. He planted a kiss on her lips. Then a thought occurred to him and he pulled back. "You're positive?"

She nodded. "The doctor's office confirmed it this morning."

"You mean when you had some errands to run in town and didn't want me to go with you?"

She nodded. "I wasn't sure. And I didn't want to get your hopes up until I knew for sure."

"I thought we agreed that there would be no secrets in our marriage."

"It wasn't a secret. I was just waiting until the right moment to tell you."

"Uh-huh." And then he started to wonder if the house was big enough.

"What are you thinking?"

"That five bedrooms might not be enough for this expanding family of ours."

"Avery, just how many babies are you planning on?"

"Oh, I don't know. But with Beth and Jordan each having a room that leaves just two spare rooms. And you never know. I've grown to like the idea of a large family."

Jillian's eyes twinkled with merriment. "I think we'll have to discuss this a lot more."

"Most definitely." He pulled her closer and gave her a proper kiss.

The End

You'll love the next book in the…

Bachelor Bake-Off series

Available now at your favorite online retailer!

About the Author

Award-winning author, Jennifer Faye pens fun, heartwarming contemporary romances with rugged cowboys, sexy billionaires and enchanting royalty. Internationally published with books translated into nine languages. She is a two-time winner of the RT Book Reviews Reviewers' Choice Award, the CataRomance Reviewers' Choice Award, named a TOP PICK author, and been nominated for numerous other awards.

Now living her dream, she resides with her very patient husband, amazing daughter (the other remarkable daughter is off chasing her own dreams) and two spoiled cats. When she's not plotting out her next romance, you can find her curled up with a mug of tea and a book.

You can learn more about Jennifer at her website jenniferfaye.com.

Thank you for reading

Sprinkled with Love

If you enjoyed this book, you can find more from all our great authors at TulePublishing.com, or from your favorite online retailer.

Made in the USA
San Bernardino, CA
23 March 2017